THE DEATH OF THE
RED KING

PAUL DOHERTY

GREENWICH EXCHANGE

WEST SUSSEX		
LIBRARIES		
200326840		
HJ	08/12/2006	
F	£16.99	
Aw 7/07 NW 03/08	FS 12/08	

Greenwich Exchange, London

The Death of the Red King © Paul Doherty 2006

First published in Great Britain in 2006
All rights reserved

This book is sold subject to the conditions that it shall not, by way of trade or otherwise, be lent, resold, hired out, or otherwise circulated without the publisher's prior consent in any form of binding or cover other than that in which it is published and without a similar condition including this condition being imposed on the subsequent publisher.

Printed and bound by Q3 Digital/Litho, Loughborough
Tel: 01509 213456
Typesetting and layout by Albion Associates, London
Tel: 020 8852 4646
Cover design by December Publications, Belfast
Tel: 028 90286559

Cover: King William II (Rufus) Shot with an Arrow, c.1300-1325
© Hermitage Image Partnerships

Greenwich Exchange website: www.greenex.co.uk

Cataloguing in Publication Data is available from the British Library.

ISBN-13: 978-1-871551-92-1
ISBN-10: 1-871551-92-7

This book is dedicated to the memory of
Geoffrey Reeve
a much loved son and brother who is greatly missed.

Contents

List of Principal Characters		vii
Main Dates		ix
I	Matins	1
	Historical Notes	13
II	Lauds	14
	Historical Notes	38
III	Prime	42
	Historical Notes	51
IV	Terce	52
	Historical Notes	93
V	Sext	95
	Historical Notes	109
VI	Nones	110
	Historical Notes	125
VII	Vespers	126
VIII	Compline	166
VII & VIII Vespers and Compline *Historical Notes*		168

List of Principal Characters

ANSELM (1022-1109) – Monk of Bec, Theologian, Philosopher, Archbishop of Canterbury (1093-1109).

EADMER – Close friend and ally of Anselm and his successor Ralph. The author of outstanding histories: *The History of Our Own Time* and his *Life of Anselm*.

WILLIAM THE CONQUEROR ('The Bastard') (1027-1087) – Son of Duke Robert and his mistress Arlette. Duke of Normandy and, after the battle of Hastings 1066, King of England.

MATHILDA (d.1083) – Wife of William the Conqueror.

ROBERT CURTHOSE – Son of the Conqueror. Duke of Normandy, Crusader. Completely out-manoeuvred by his brothers, William and Henry.

WILLIAM ('Rufus') (c.1058-1100) – The Red King, son of the Conqueror and Mathilda. King of England.

HENRY I (d.1135) – King of the English, brother to the Red King, son of the Conqueror.

MATHILDA ('Edith') (1080-1118) – Wife/Queen of Henry I, daughter of Malcolm III of Scotland and Margaret, descendant of the Saxon royal line.

LANFRANC (d.1089) – Benedictine monk. Archbishop of Canterbury. Close confidant of the Conqueror, patron and friend of Anselm.

HAROLD GODWINSON – A member of the powerful Godwin family. He seized the Crown after the death of the Confessor. He was defeated and killed at Hastings (1066).

RANULF FLAMBARD (d.1128) – Bishop of Durham. Chief Minister of William Rufus deposed and imprisoned by Henry I for a while.

WALTER TIREL – Lord of Poix. Owner of Langham in Essex. Husband of Adelicia de Clare.

ROBERT DE BEAUMONT (d. 1118) – Count of Meulan. One of the Conqueror's companions, Chief Councillor to William the Red King and Henry I.

HENRY DE BEAUMONT – Earl of Warwick, brother of the above.

FITZHAIMO (d. 1108) – Norman baron, powerful in the south-west and along the Welsh March.

SERLO OF GLOUCESTER – Benedictine Monk, formerly of Avranches and Sées. Abbot of St Peter's, Gloucester. Serlo sent warning to William the Red King of his impending doom.

HELIAS LA FLÈCHE – Count of Maine. Opponent of William the Red King.

Main Dates

1058   William the Red King born.

1065   Death of Edward the Confessor. William of Normandy challenges Harold Godwinson for the English throne.

1066   October, Battle of Senlac (Hastings). Duke William defeats and kills Harold Godwinson.

1087   William, the Red, becomes King.

1088   William crushes rebellions and uprisings in England.

1089   Lanfranc, Archbishop of Canterbury dies. No successor is appointed.

1090   William the Red King holds a Great Council at Winchester regarding a projected invasion of Normandy.

1091   William invades Normandy, defeats his brother, Robert, who unites with him to defeat their younger brother Henry.

1093   The Red King falls grievously ill at Gloucester. He vows to reform if he recovers, he appoints Anselm as Archbishop of Canterbury.

1094	Quarrel between the Red King and Anselm begins over control of the Church.
1096	Duke Robert pledges Normandy to his brother for 10,000 marks to finance Robert's participation in the First Crusade.
1097	Anselm, unable to resolve his dispute with William, goes into exile.
1097	William the Red King goes to war with Philip of France.
1097-99	The war in France continues. William invades both Maine and the Vexin.
1099	25th December: William holds his Christmas court at Gloucester.
1100	William moves to Westminster and then onto Winchester and the New Forest. 2nd August: William the Red King killed in the New Forest.

I

Matins

The Sons of Ephraim, armed with the bow.
(Psalm 77)

My master does not like to talk of demons. Anselm of Bec, Archbishop of Canterbury, smiles and hides his face when any of the good brothers talk about devilish horns and eyes which spark and burn like fiery coals through the darkness of this world. Anselm gently reminds me that Lucifer, the Morning Star before he fell from Paradise, was a great-winged spirit of living flame.

"Two wings," Anselm commented, "one of love, the other of intellect. Lucifer fell, my dear Eadmer – " Anselm pushed his face closer, " – because he relied solely on the wing of intellect."

We were talking in the herbarium of St Augustine's Abbey in Canterbury. A beautiful warm summer's day, bathing in its golden glow the full-bloomed shrubs and flowers. Across the herb garden drifted the different sounds of the Abbey: the choir practising in the church nave, chanting some melodious psalm; the ringing of a distant bell; the patter of sandaled feet; the clatter of pots from the butteries and kitchens. Nearby old Brother Regnaut dozed on his bench, in the shade of a beautiful copper beech planted in the centre of the herbarium, its branches spread out to shield the shoots from the glare of the sun. The old man was talking to himself, as he often did, about the blood-soaked battlefield at Senlac. In his glory days Regnaut had been a housecarl in the retinue of Harold Godwinson. He had been present that far-off sombre October day, when the arrows fell like hail and the Saxon shield wall buckled and broke. Godwinson had staggered back with an arrow in his face and the Conqueror had broken through with mace, sword and axe, shattering bone and brain in showers of blood. A day when dreams had died and new ones were born. That was a lifetime away. Regnaut, after the battle, had become a lay-brother to housel his soul and shrive his sins. Now he sat snug, fitfully dreaming amidst the summer flowers, lulled to sleep by the psalms of chanting monks. He'd wake soon enough to smack his lips at the prospect of mead-cup or a flagon of frothy ale. Poor Regnaut! On that day, the Feast of Mary Magdalene, Father Anselm, Archbishop of Canterbury, 'Legatus a latere' of his Holiness in Rome, pointed at the snoring lay-brother.

"A generation gone," he murmured, "all gone to God. Godwin's flaxen-haired, warrior son, Harold; William the bastard. And yet ..." Anselm paused, bony fingers grasping his stomach.

I gazed helplessly back. Father Anselm is truly dying; he is weakened by some malady within, a malignancy of the humours. Many years have passed. What? Some 74 since his birth at Val d'Aosta? In that time, like some fiery comet, Anselm has seared the skies of our souls. Anselm the theologian, the politician, the mystic, the contemplative, the recluse, the monk, the archbishop, the defender of the Church, the scourge of kings and, for me, close friend, spiritual father – and I to him? Eadmer, his faithful secretary. Father Anselm has aged. This certainly shows in his narrowed face beneath matted, white hair yet he remains luminous-eyed and merry-mouthed, still deeply involved in problems of logic, philosophy and theology, those great loves which absorb his keen intellect. He continues to wrestle with such problems delineated in his 'De Casu Diaboli', trying to reconcile the mysteries of God's full knowledge with man's free will. On that particular day Father Anselm had decided to resolve another problem, one from our past. He leaned on my arm and pointed his walking stick towards the flowering arbour at the end of the herbarium walk.

"Let's go there," he murmured, "so we won't disturb Brother Regnaut. I feel tired, Eadmer, tired by my journeys, my fighting, my thinking." He stared up at the sky. "Soon," he added as we edged along the path, "I will be summoned to attend the Easter Court of the Lord Jesus and yet," he sighed as he sat down in the arbour, "one doom, one death – ", he paused to cough, " – still weighs heavily on me." He continued as if talking to himself. "Soon, in ten days, his anniversary occurs once again. I have already begun to chant the Requiem Masses." Anselm sat, one vein-streaked hand half raised, staring intently towards the Abbey church.

"Requiem dona ei Domine ..." he murmured. "Eternal rest grant to him O Lord and let perpetual light shine upon him ..."

"Father, about whom are you talking?"

"Why, Brother, the King!" He laughed softly, "William the Red – Rufus."

"The Red King!" I gasped. I recalled what I had written in my own *History of Recent Events in England*. About how we had both reacted to the news of the Red King's sudden and brutal death in the New Forest on the sun-filled evening of 2nd August, the morrow of Lammas, in the year of Our Lord, 1100. At the time Father Anselm and I were sheltering in exile at Lyons after my master's bitter quarrel with that same King.

"What did you write of the Red King's death?" Anselm asked gently. "You know, in that passage where you describe the death of old Pope Urban and the accession of his successor, Paschal. Read it again for me, Eadmer."

I picked up my leather chancery sack, opened it, and took out my own *History of Recent Events in England*. I leafed through the freshly-scrubbed, clearly-written pages until I found the passage Anselm had asked for.

3

"'Meanwhile'," I commenced reading, "'a rumour spread through the various countries that Pope Urban had died. In fact, he'd died before he'd received a reply to Anselm's case which he was expecting from the King of England. When the Pope's death came to the ears of King William, he exclaimed: "The hatred of God rest upon whoever cares a rat for that!"'" I continued reading my finger following the words. "'The King went on to ask, "But the new Pope, what sort of man is he?" When he received the reply how, in some aspects, the new Pope was like Archbishop Anselm – '" I glanced up. My master was nodding gently to himself. I returned to the manuscript "' – the King replied, "By the Face of God, if he's like that, he is no good, so let him keep strictly to himself, for the Pope shall not get the upper hand of me this time, to that I take my oath! I've gained my freedom and I shall do freely as I like." William the Red King believed that not even the Pope of this whole world could have any jurisdiction in his Kingdom unless it was by his permission, but how he behaved after this is not the place to write of here, as I must hasten on to deal with other matters …'"

I paused as if listening to the buzz of the bees as they plundered the flowers.

"Continue," Anselm whispered.

"'But the King'," I read, returning to the manuscript, "'was not long allowed to enjoy the liberty of which he had boasted. Less than a year elapsed before he lost it altogether, being struck down by an unexpected and sudden death. On the second day of the following August, after having breakfast – '" I glanced up, " – I wrote that at the time, but I now realise I was wrong, William went hunting much later. Anyway," I continued, "'he rode out to the forest to hunt, and was there struck by an arrow which pierced his heart. Impenitent and unshriven, he died instantly and was immediately forsaken by everyone. Now, whether as some say, that arrow struck him in its flight or, as the majority declare, he stumbled and, so falling right upon it, met his death, is a question we do not think necessary to raise. It is sufficient to realise that, by the judgement of God, William, King of England was stricken down and slain.'"

"So pride comes before a fall." Anselm rested his hands on his walking stick and stared at a small fountain carved in a shape of a sea monster which stood at the far end of the herbarium.

"Continue, Brother," he urged, "read what you wrote when we received the news."

I leafed over a page and found the place. I deliberately turned to a passage just before that and, although I heard Anselm tut-tut, I insisted on reading it.

"'The King'," I declared, "'proceeded step-by-step so far in his evil ways as those who were present with him by day and by night bear witness. The Red King never got up in the morning, or went to bed at night, without seeming a worse man than when he last went to bed, or got up. So, since the King refused to be disciplined by ill fortune, or to be led to right doing by good fortune, but continued to brunt his raging fury to the detriment of all good men, the Just Judge, by a death sharp and swift, cut his life from this world.'"

"Very good, very good," Anselm whispered, "but that passage, Eadmer, read it to me."

"'In the second year after he'd come from Rome to Lyons, which was the third year of our exile, Father Anselm was spending three days at the monastery of 'La Chaise Dieu'. Two monks came to him, one from Canterbury, the other from Bec, bringing news of the death of King William, about whom I have already spoken. This news came as a great shock to Father Anselm. He was so overcome that he wept most bitterly. We were greatly surprised to see him so affected, but he, his voice broken – '" I ignored the sob from beside me, "' – declared the very truth from which no servant of God can rightly stray, that if it had been possible to choose, he would have much preferred that he himself had suffered this death rather than the King.'"

I closed the manuscript and stared down the sun-filled path. Anselm sat, head bowed, sobbing quietly to himself. I don't know whether he was praying for himself or for the Red King but, now and again I caught the words "Miserere, have mercy".

"Listen, Brother, and listen well." Anselm lifted his head. "William the Red King was much despised by clerics and monks – " he paused, chewing his lower lip, " – but he was like any good tree in God's orchard bearing all kinds of fruit, some rotten – ", he turned and stared at me, " – some ripe to fullness. Every man born of woman has to die: kings, princes, priests – we are no more than grass in the field, here today, gone tomorrow, yet we all live in God's eyes."

"So Father …?"

Anselm edged closer still, staring down at the fountain, "Was that particular tree," he asked slowly, "cruelly hewed before its time?"

"Father," I interrupted, "why now?"

"Silentium et Sapientia," Anselm responded. "Silence and wisdom are close brothers. Over the years I have striven to be silent and wise yet I have reflected deeply. Accordingly I have, my dear Brother – ", he patted me on the arm, " – invited them all here. They'll arrive soon."

"Who, Father, who are you talking about?"

"Let me state my hypothesis," Anselm replied. "Eight summers ago, in the year of Our Lord's birth 1100, on Thursday, 2nd August, William the Red King, late in the evening, not in the morning as you've written, Eadmer, decided to go hunting in the New Forest – that vast tract of woodland covering almost an entire shire; a place of goblins and elves. The Forest, or so say the Chronicles, is a dark, green, velvet mantle which hides marshes, swamps and quagmires. According to local lore, the Hidden Ones, the People of the Night who held this Kingdom long before the Romans came, shelter there. It is the home and castle of the tusked boar and the sharp-antlered deer." Anselm put his stick down and pressed his hands together. "Thickets so dense, brambles so sharp, you'd think the ancient gods had built it as a final fortress to protect themselves, and yet," he added, "they also say – the chroniclers, the gossips of our time – that the New Forest was really the work of William the Bastard. He destroyed villages, hamlets, cottages and even churches, because the Conqueror and his sons loved the red deer more than any children."

"Is that true, Father?"

"Perhaps." Anselm turned, light blue eyes scrutinising me. His severe face was lined and grey, but those eyes, seemed like those of a young man questioning everything he saw.

"What are you implying, Father?"

"William the Red King, son of the great Conqueror and Queen Mathilda, was killed on that Lammas morrow." He glanced away.

"An accident!" I retorted. "A mere accident! Walter Tirel, Lord of Poix, a visitor from Poitou in France, was hunting with the Red King when the sun was setting. Walter loosed a shaft and, by mere chance, hit the King. Tirel was a royal friend, a boon companion of the Prince he accidentally killed."

"Has Tirel said that?"

I went to answer but held my peace. My master enjoyed that unique skill, of posing a simple question which demands careful reflection before any reply. Eleven years earlier, when Anselm and William the Red King had quarrelled over the power of the Pope to appoint bishops, as well as Anselm's rights as Archbishop of Canterbury, matters came to an abrupt head. My master was visited by a delegation of royal emissaries led by Robert Beaumont, Count of Meulan. They approached my master to remonstrate with him over his obduracy towards the King. He responded with one simple question – how did his loyalty to the Bishop of Rome conflict with his loyalty to the King?

If they'd replied it did, they would have to prove it, whilst Anselm in his defence, would have merely quoted Scripture and the canons of the church with which they could not disagree. On the other hand, if they'd said his loyalties didn't conflict, Anselm would have merely asked why then were they bothering him? They couldn't answer his question then and, 11 years later, still could not muster a suitable reply. It was the same in that herb garden with the grey paving stones baking under the sun, the bees hunting lazily amongst the flowers, above which white-winged butterflies floated like the souls of little children.

"And Tirel?" he insisted.

"Father," I replied, "you know Sir Walter. He has dined with you …"

"Has he ever said," Anselm persisted, "has he ever confessed to that accident?"

"It was God's will," he groaned in exasperation, "that the Red King be punished for his sins, his hideous crimes against Holy Mother Church."

"So Brother," Anselm teased, "God willed Rufus to commit such crimes with the full knowledge that he would punish him."

I glared in mock anger at my master. He just laughed, a soft, merry sound like that of a boy at a funny jape performed by some mummer or jester.

"Master!" I exclaimed.

"I know, I know." Anselm lifted his hand and stared at the ave beads wrapped round his fingers. He made its small wooden crucifix swing before his eyes.

"The eternal problem," he mused, "we have free will, but if God knows what we are going to choose, is it really free? And if we choose evil, is God party to that? Do you know, Brother, in my thoughts on that problem, I turn like a swallow twisting under God's sky, yet I cannot resolve the issue." He smiled. "But remember my question about Tirel! Come." He plucked at my sleeve and, hand resting on my arm, we made our way down the path into the cloister. The good brothers were sitting in their carrels taking full advantage of the light, the air reeked of parchment, ink and perfumed sand. The screech of quills mingled with the murmuring of the brothers. Across the garth drifted the voice of the Choir Cantor: "Lavabo manus meas inter innocentes" – "I will wash my hands amongst the innocent".

Anselm stopped walking, head cocked as if listening, before leading me down the stone galleries to his own austere chamber. It is little more than a cell with lime-washed walls. On one of these hung a crude crucifix above a prie-dieu; a high desk stood under the window with a matching chair; in the far corner a palliasse bed and next to it a heavy oaken robing chest and an iron-bound coffer. On a small table in the centre of the cell was a tray of food and wine, still untouched, the servants had brought it for my master's midday meal. He followed my gaze.

"Too much," he whispered, rubbing his stomach. He went across to the heavy chest, opened it, took out a set of leather pannier bags and placed them at his feet. "Brother Eadmer," he smiled at me, "I have a great favour to ask. In a few days time, on the morrow of Lammas, I have invited the King, his beloved wife Mathilda – " Anselm paused as if regretting the tinge of sarcasm in his voice, " – Robert Beaumont, Count of Meulan, his brother, Henry Earl of Warwick, Lord Fitzhaimo and ..." he screwed up his eyes, staring at the door.

"And who, Father?"

Anselm turned and peered at the shaft of light pouring through the needle-thin window like a ray of God's grace into an empty soul.

"Robert of Normandy," he murmured.

"The King's brother!" I exclaimed. "But he is in prison!"

"House arrest," Anselm corrected, lifting a bony finger. "Comfortable confinement at the White Tower near London. I have insisted they must all be my guests."

"Why, Father?"

"I told them I am going to die, so I need to see them."

"But?" I gazed heavy-hearted at him.

"It's not a lie," Anselm retorted. "In a short while we are all going to lie side by side whilst our souls journey on to God." He took a step closer. "In the end," he whispered hoarsely, "I want to know the truth. Listen." He kicked the leather panniers at his feet. "I have sent Ivo and Reginald." Anselm shook his head in amusement as he always did when he mentioned his two messengers: Merry Jacks, Will-of-the-Wisps who liked nothing better than galloping round the countryside on this errand or that. "You must have noticed how they've been gone some months? Well, they have been good scholars," Anselm chuckled. "Sent to that monastery, this abbey or cathedral library. They have carried my seal and asked for copies of all the different chronicles which have been written about the death of the Red King. Monks." He cleared his throat. "We monks reap the harvest of gossip and rumour, the whisper and the scandal as well as the true cause of things. Ivo and Reginald have collected all the scurrilous chatter about our late but, sorrowfully, not lamented King."

"Hot cinders of gossip," I riposted, "glowing coals of scandal. Master, as you've said, the Red King was not liked by churchmen."

"Or by you, Eadmer." Anselm lifted a hand. "And yet in truth, kings are not crowned to be liked but to rule." He rubbed his hands together. "To rule," he repeated staring down at the ground, "not to be killed by a cruel arrow."

"God's vengeance," was all I could reply. I was intrigued by my master's absorption with this matter and went to question him but Anselm just shook his head. He lifted one of the panniers, undid the buckles and moved into the ray of light so that he could sift more easily among the contents. Whilst he did so, he gently hummed the tune of a hymn, 'Ubi Caritas, ibi Amor' – 'Where charity is, so is love.' He plucked out a piece of parchment and went across to the window.

"Listen to this, Eadmer – the text of a sermon by Fulchered, formerly a monk of Sees, first Abbot of Shrewsbury. This is his homily delivered on the Feast of St Peter ad Vincula, 1st August 1100, in the Cathedral Abbey of St Peter of Gloucester, the very day before the Red King was slain." He glanced up and pointed at me. "Remember that, Eadmer, Gloucester! Anyway – " Anselm moved to catch the light better, " – this is what one chronicler writes about that sermon.

'On 1st of August, the Feast of St Peter in Chains was celebrated at the monastery of Gloucester in the presence of a huge congregation comprising both royalty and clergy. On that occasion, Fulchered, a zealous monk, the first Abbot of Shrewsbury and an eloquent student of the Holy Scripture, was chosen from the senior monks to climb into the pulpit and preach the sermon to the populace on the saving power of God. Fulchered did not spare his congregation. He did not confine himself to spiritual matters, but openly condemned the public violations of the Divine Law and, as if filled with the spirit of prophecy, declared: "England has been given over to reprobates for destruction and now the land reeks of foul lusts. The whole body of our Kingdom is spotted as if with a leprosy of evil in its many forms; from head to foot it is wholly infected with a moral sickness. Over this strange landscape, pride prowls everywhere and tramples all things underfoot, even as one may put it, the stars in the sky. Lust pollutes bodies, and voracious greed devours all within its reach. However, a day of judgement is at hand, those who pretend to be women will reign for not much longer. The Lord God is about to carry out judgement against the enemies of his spouse. He will strike, as he did against Moab and Edom, with the sword of terrible vengeance. He will overthrow the mountains of Gilboa with a horrid disturbance. The anger of God will no longer spare sinners. Already the angels of heaven rage against the Sons of Iniquity. Look, the bow of Divine Anger is bent against the wicked, and God's arrow is swift to inflict its wound. The arrow is already from the quiver, it will strike suddenly, let every wise man who hears this warning avoid the blow by mending his life ..."'"

"Strange." Anselm placed the piece of manuscript down on the table beside the tray of food. "Strange isn't it, how on Lammas Day, the Feast of St Peter in Chains, the very day before King William was killed, a Benedictine abbot talks of God's bow being pulled back? He refers to the death of King Saul in the Old Testament, killed by arrows on the heights of Gilboa. A coincidence, Eadmer? Did Fulchered really have the gift of foresight or was it something else?"

Confused, I could only stand and let the coldness creep across my skin. My master, Anselm, Monk of Bec, Archbishop of Canterbury, was following his own dark path.

"What are you saying?" I spluttered, "Why all this?"

"Why not?" he retorted, coming forward. "When Rufus was killed, I burst into tears. I openly wished I could have given my life for his." He scratched his head and pointed down at the panniers. "Collect all this Brother, study them, draw the story out. Compile all the accounts. Let me also know what happened in the first two years following the Red King's death. Collect and study it all. Spin it out like yarn to make good cloth. What really did happen in the New Forest on that August day? Why was William Rufus killed? Whom do the chroniclers say was responsible and how did he die?" He glanced up fierce-eyed and plucked the front of my gown. "Who did loose that shaft at the King's heart as the sun set, the shadows lengthened and the devil came hunting? I must know Brother Eadmer, before I die! William was my King, I was his Archbishop. Oh yes, we were enemies, at least in the eyes of men, though not in the eyes of God. His father entrusted that Prince to Archbishop Lanfranc to look after. I am Lanfranc's successor. I have a charge to answer, a stewardship for which I must account. When the Hours of God arrive ..." He paused as if not wishing to illuminate what that was a reference to. "Yes." He shook his head vigorously. "When the Hours of God arrive so will the time of truth ..."

I

Matins

Historical Notes

The historical sources for Anselm and Eadmer are fairly plentiful. Both were Benedictine monks. Anselm had gained an outstanding reputation for sanctity, asceticism and the purity of his logic, displayed in great theological works such as *Cur Deus Homo* – 'Why God became Man'. The key work here is Eadmer's *Historia Novorum in Anglia* – 'Recent History of Events in England' edited by G. Bonsaquet, (The Cresset Press, 1964). R.W. Southern's *Anselm and his Biographer* (Cambridge, 1963) provides a brilliant analysis of the close, intimate relationship between these two men. Anselm was a genius, a man of deep spirituality who leaned on the more practical Eadmer. Indeed it is difficult to assess Anselm except through Eadmer's eyes, though J.M. Rigg's, *Anselm* (Methuen, 1896) attempts this. The most objective source for Anselm, his relationship with the Red King and the general background events, are provided by that incorrigible Autolycus "a snapper-up of mere trifles", Oderic Vitalis, *Ecclesiastical History* (Oxford, 1975), Volume V, comprising books ix and x. For Abbot Fulchered's sermon – Oderic Vitalis: Book V, pp. 286-88.

II

Lauds

He drew me from the deadly pit.
(Psalm 39)

Around the time the Red King died so violently, the blood pouring out of a black wound in his chest, all forms of portents and omens were seen throughout the Kingdom: a sacred well in Berkshire bubbled blood; the weather grew foul; the moon turned to blood, and a comet appeared with straggling light as if it had sprouted a beard. According to the Chronicles: Satan stalked the land and appeared in woodlands and lonely wastes, warning both Saxon and Norman of the coming doom; how the Warrior of Hell had sprung into the world, spear poised, shield raised; how all the powers of hell had followed to plot the destruction of the Red King as it had been prophesised by Merlin the Warlock. I, Eadmer, read such omens, such accounts as I sat in that lonely chamber at St Augustine's and studied what my master had collected from the different scriptoria, chanceries and libraries of monasteries, abbeys and cathedrals throughout the Kingdom. However, before I turn that dark corner let me say matters did not begin that way.

    William Rufus was the younger son of little Mathilda of Boulogne, wife of the Bastard, the great Conqueror, William of Normandy. By primogeniture, neither the Crown nor the Duchy of Normandy belonged to Rufus. He had an elder brother, Richard, also killed whilst hunting in the New Forest, [a matter to which I

The Death of the Red King

will return later] as well as Robert Curthose or 'Robert the Short', the Crusader, amiable and reckless, who in the end lost everything, including his liberty. However, 'In initio' – 'in the beginning' it was as follows: William the Bastard struck down Harold Godwinson at his God-given victory on Senlac Hill. For the next 21 years the Conqueror struggled to bring England under his sword whilst striving to fend off the hordes of two-legged wolves who fought to devour Normandy when his back was turned. Leading this pack was Philip I of France who had no love for the Bastard. In his latter years the Great Conqueror had aged. He had certainly changed from the athletic warrior. In appearance, the Conqueror was of medium height, of great muscular strength, his face had always been harsh but, by the year of his death, had turned sterner still. He had also grown a paunch as fat and heavy as a bulging wine-skin. Philip of France, stung by the Conqueror's outstanding success, jibed that his opponent looked more like a woman in child-bearing than a soldier.

"By the Splendour and Resurrection of God," the great Conqueror had retorted with one of his favourite oaths, "if that is the case, I'll light a hundred thousand candles for my churching."

In the war which followed, the Conqueror invaded the Vexin – that narrow strip of land which would have sped the Norman like a whirling shaft into the heart of Philip's dominions and the city of Paris. During that fierce struggle, William burnt the city of Nantes, putting it to the torch, the fierce fire turning it into a living hell. William was parading through the smoke-charred ruins when his war-horse, stung by flying sparks, reared violently and the hard saddle-horn pierced the King's huge belly like a dagger, inflicting a deadly wound. He was taken to Rouen. When the physicians were unable to staunch the wound or halt the putrefaction which followed, he was conveyed to the nearby monastic cell of St Gervaise. The Lord Jesus gave William the Bastard five weeks to prepare for his death, so he gathered his sons to divide his empire. His heirs arrived more concerned with their private interests than the common good, cunning messengers with twisted words had sown seeds of dispute in already fertile soil. William and Robert, the two eldest sons, were already enemies and had clashed in open warfare. William Rufus had supported his father when Robert, reckless and footloose, had rebelled against the crown. The Conqueror had no great love for Robert, albeit the apple of his mother's eye, though in the end he left Normandy to Robert as a Dukedom fief. England was a different matter. To the dying King, England was a result of a conquest carried through by the murder of thousands of innocent people and every imaginable sin. The Bastard was unwilling to bequeath that Kingdom to anyone but God. However, he was finally persuaded to give it to Rufus, thinking that he would bring peace and glory to his new kingdom. To his youngest son Henry, the dying king left five thousand pounds in silver, though, according to the chroniclers, his father predicted that one day he would own everything. However, there again, that is the hidden talent of monastic writers, hindsight makes prophets of us all! In fairness, Henry also had seisin of his mother's property in both Normandy and England. Once all this was completed, the Bastard immediately despatched Rufus to England bearing letters to Lanfranc, Archbishop of Canterbury, ordering him to crown his son as quickly as possible. Wise advice! The wolves were already gathering, the kites and buzzards circling above the new King. William Rufus had not even left Normandy when messengers on the fleetest horses brought news of his father's death. Rufus did not turn back but hurried on to England. He was spared the horror of his father's burial at Caen when the already corpulent corpse, swollen by evil humours, was pushed into a sarcophagus too small for it. The cadaver burst like a rotten apple, fouled the air and drove mourners from the church. William the new King, more concerned with the living, reached England safely. First he rode, swift as an arrow, to Winchester to secure the treasury, seal it with his own insignia and swear its keepers to loyalty. Afterwards he hastened into London to bring the news of his father's death to great Lanfranc who was almost shocked to his own death by the account of what had happened in Normandy.

On 26th September in the year of Our Lord, 1087, William the Red was crowned, christened and hallowed as King. The great men bowed before him and took the oath; all was completed and sanctified by Lanfranc. The crown-wearing confirmed William's position, but what manner of man was the Red King? In appearance he was tough and pot-bellied with the muscular arms of an archer and the strong legs of a horse rider. He was broad-browed, with eyes of different colours, flecked with specks of light. His hair was yellow like wet corn, parted down the middle. He grew a moustache and beard, his jaw jutted out aggressively, his thick-set lips stumbled and stammered, but when he lost his temper, a frequent occurrence, he could shout and bawl a litany of curses as colourful as any uttered by his father. His most favourite oath was, "By the Holy face of Lucca", although he often indulged in other blasphemies. Violent and swollen with anger, William Rufus could also be generous and jovial – especially with his soldiers. He was very vain, especially about his sense of dress. A chronicler tells a particular story illustrating this: once, when a chamberlain produced a new pair of boots for him, William enquired how much they had cost? "Three shillings!" the man replied. "You son of a whore! Since when does a king wear boots as cheap as that," the Red King roared, "go and buy me some for a mark of silver." When the chamberlain hurried off and returned with an even cheaper pair which he falsely claimed cost a mark, the King declared, "True, these are more fitting for a royal majesty!"

Such is the vanity of vanities of princes and yet, although he loved ostentation, jewellery and sumptuous feasts, the Red King's greatest desire was the chase, so wolf-hunters and deer-men were constantly in his company. Of his courage or valour in war there can be no doubt. One example will suffice: in the year before he died, William was hunting in the New Forest just after the Whitsun celebrations, when a messenger arrived from Normandy bearing the news that Helias La Flèche, Count of Maine, had invaded William's territories and was besieging Le Mans and how gallows had been set up to hang knights, sergeants and other servants of the King. William hastily broke the seal of the letter and read the details which simply confirmed what the messenger had said. Helias was besieging the King's city of Le Mans, most of this had been put to the torch, with only the loyal garrison holding out in the central donjon. The King responded immediately. He had been sitting at a table enjoying a meal but sprang up, took his fleetest horse and galloped to the coast. Others followed, trying to persuade him to wait and summon an army. "Let's find out. Who will follow me?" The King shouted back. "Do you think I won't collect troops? If I know my men they'll fly to me even across raging seas." Despite the stormy weather and with only a few companions, the Red King reached the coast to find the wind contrary to a sailing and the sea very rough. He commandeered a ship and persuaded the reluctant captain to take them across, joking that he'd never heard of a king being lost at sea.

"Cast off sailor!" he shouted, "you'll see the wind and sea will do all I want." Guided through the storm by God, according to one Chronicle, the Red King safely reached the port of Touques where he was greeted by a crowd of curious locals. Seizing a local priest's horse, William mounted, mustered troops and made his way to Le Mans, where he drove Helias out: an eloquent testament to the Red King's personal courage.

Nevertheless, the King's private life was scandalous, scarred by sins as red as blood and moral stains as dark as the blackest night. When the great Lanfranc was alive, the Archbishop acted as a rein on William's natural passions, but once Lanfranc passed on to his immortal reward, the stallion ran free and loose. The Red King never had a lawful wife but enjoyed a host of concubines.

According to the Chronicles, as well as the evidence collected by my master, William gave himself up insatiably to obscene fornications and repeated adulteries. Stained with such sins, he set a damnable example of debauchery to his subjects. At the Red King's court, young men grew their hair freshly combed like girls, and acted the part with roaming eyes and insidious gestures. They pranced about in girlish steps, their clothes luxurious, their shoes adorned with pointed and curled toes. Young courtiers aped women in the soft movements of their bodies and walked with mincing steps. The King brought in men who were weak, effeminate and violated the chastity of others. A band of transvestites, effeminates, and harlots of either sex transformed his court into a brothel of catamites rather than a place of majesty. Sodomy and adultery were rife. Improper fashions became common, with tight-fitting shirts and tunics, elegant robes and mantles boasting voluminous sleeves. In a word, men dressed like women. They wore their hair long at the back like whores, the centre parted, baring their foreheads like thieves, their abundant locks crimped and tendered, curled with tongs and caught up in a headband and covered with a cap. The weakness of the flesh was there for all to see. My master, Anselm – and I know this without consulting the Chronicles – bitterly opposed this. Before we went into exile, Anselm raised the vexed question of sodomy with the King in person. He demanded that both Crown and Church co-operate in convening a General Council to prevent the whole Kingdom from becoming no different from Sodom and Gomorrah. The King refused and this issue became another burning ember in the quarrel between Father Anselm and the Red King. My Master eventually retaliated. In his Lenten homilies for that year, he inveighed vehemently against such perverse practices. He refused to distribute the ashes on Ash Wednesday, or the Eucharist, to any courtier who persisted in their lewdness.

    Beside his concupiscence, William was also greedy for wealth. When bishoprics, abbacies and other ecclesiastical offices fell vacant, the Red King refused to appoint or confirm a successor but delayed for as long as he could, so that the revenues of the Holy Mother Church were immediately diverted to his own bulging treasuries. When he did appoint, William chose from those beloved amongst his minions. The leader of his coven, a veritable imp of Satan, was Ranulf Flambard who advised the Red King on all his wicked policies, especially the ravishing of church revenues. Flambard was directly responsible for the Archbishopric of Canterbury being left vacant so the King could plunder its revenues for four barren years before God and his Saints intervened.

The Red King fell grievously sick at Gloucester in the year of Our Lord 1093 and vowed to reform if he were cured. God be praised he was and, in fulfilment of this pledge, Anselm was appointed as the Archbishop of Canterbury. However, once he'd recovered his health, the King returned to his wickedness as a dog to his vomit! He threw off the blessed Anselm's counsels as one would a cloak and returned to his lecherous ways. Flambard encouraged him in such mischief. This minion of Satan was the son of Thurston, a village priest in the Norman diocese of Bayeux. In appearance Flambard was of medium height, short-headed with a powerful protuberant jaw, a sloping forehead and beetling brows over eyes which smouldered with all the fires of villainy. Ranulf had swiftly climbed the tree of preferment through artful flattery. He stoked the King's vanity with the tinder of avarice and the torch of iniquity. He was bold, forthright and of ready wit. He was well named Flambard, a veritable fire, a tongue of flame shot out from the very blackness of hell. He was an invincible pleader in the courts. Extravagant in words and deeds, Flambard would defend the King's rights as if defending a castle against avowed traitors. Flambard purchased ecclesiastical offices, including the Bishopric of Durham for £1000. He was hardly fitted for such high office, being a pastor more interested in the fleece than looking after the flock. He had a mistress, Aelfgifu of

Huntingdon by whom he had a number of children. He later married her off to a burgess of that town, although Ranulf continued to lodge with her in his journeys up and down the kingdom. He loved nothing better than to tease men of God. On one occasion as Bishop of Durham, Ranulf forced the monks to eat with him in the Hall, where he not only provided the monks with meat, which was forbidden on fast days, but ordered it to be served by maids dressed unbecomingly in tight short clothes, their hair hanging free down their backs.

Many men hated Flambard, but his courage withstood them and pleased his master. In the year of Our Lord 1091 Ranulf was proclaimed King's Chaplain and exercised regal authority during the Red King's absence from the realm. In that very year, one of Ranulf's vassals named Gerard, a member of his household who was as much dedicated to food, drink and lechery as his master, was suborned by Ranulf's enemies in a plot to kidnap and kill the royal favourite. Disembarking from a small boat at the palace quayside near Westminster, Flambard met Gerard. He claimed to have been sent by Maurice, Bishop of London, who allegedly lay at death's door in his manor at Stepney and wanted Ranulf to visit him. Not suspecting any evil, Ranulf boarded a boat with his notary and a few other servants. However, he became suspicious when Gerard steered down mid-river straight for the sea, where they reached a cog full of armed men waiting for their arrival. Ranulf, realising he was about to be kidnapped, threw his chancery ring overboard, his notary followed suit. He cast away the royal seals to prevent their use by the conspirators who could have been used them to approve writs and so release treasure. Ranulf and his companions were bundled aboard, imprisoned in the prow while his captors debated how to kill them.

Two sailors were chosen by lot to do the deed either by casting Ranulf overboard or dashing his brains out, in return they would have all his fine clothes. However the two sailors quarrelled over who should have Flambard's mantle and this delayed matters until nightfall when a violent storm blew in from the south and the ship, much damaged, was driven back up the Thames. The crew now believed that they were stricken by God's anger and the second-in-command offered Ranulf his support. He, in turn, called upon his traitorous vassal Gerard to observe his former loyalty and promised him lavish rewards if he spared his life. In the end the captain of the ship intervened. Terrified by Flambard's authority and seduced by his promises, he agreed to liberate his captives. The ship returned to London, docking in the Thames. The captain even entertained Flambard at his house before realising the full danger of what he'd done and, collecting his possessions, fled abroad. Ranulf immediately left the house and called out the City Watch to defend him. When the Red King heard all this, he was delighted. Impressed by Ranulf's courage, he became more devoted than ever to promoting him.

Another fiend of hell was Gerard, Royal Clerk, first made Bishop of Hereford, then Archbishop of York. Nothing proves William's determination to reward members of his coven than Gerard's personality. He was a man least suited to high office and certainly not dedicated to religion. Gerard the Clerk feared neither God nor man. He concentrated solely on one verse of scripture: "pay no heed for tomorrow", for Gerard amassed wealth whenever he could. He had lived a depraved, debauched life ever since childhood. Once he was made Archbishop of York, he plotted to make his friends and servants communicants and servants of Satan. He ordered his chamberlain to bring him a pig and, when he did, the chamberlain was told to withdraw. He became suspicious, so he hid and spied on the Archbishop. He could scarcely believe what he saw and heard. Gerard talked to an invisible demon uttering unspeakable words, then saw him, on the demon's instruction, carry the pig out to the palace lavatories and worship it. The chamberlain fled, but when recalled, Gerard ordered him to invite a large number of guests to a feast and from that pig make sufficient starters for the whole company so that everyone would partake of it. However, the chamberlain, now terrified, killed the pig, buried it in the palace grounds and prepared another for the banquet. The invisible demon informed Gerard and the chamberlain fled, beating off the swordsmen who were sent to arrest him. Gerard's brother Peter was even worse. A royal chaplain, Peter openly confessed to being impregnated by a man and died of a monstrous growth. So evil was his reputation, he was buried outside the cemetery like a donkey, unworthy of consecrated ground.

The Red King's relationship with his own two brothers, Robert and Henry, was equally dark and contemptuous. Both rebelled against him and both were crushed. Robert the elder was nicknamed Curthose because of his short stature. In manner he was mild and as changeable as a feather in the wind. Some chroniclers claim that the Red King and his brother Robert made a treaty in the year 1093 by which the Red King named his elder brother as his heir to England, but others dismiss this as mere fable. Robert was taken up with a passion for the Crusade preached by Pope Urban at Clermont, so in 1096 he mortgaged Normandy to William for five years in return for 10,000 marks which he used to travel to Outremer. Many men thought Robert would not return. However in 1099, Robert, for the first time in his life, surprised both his own household and family. He left the Holy Land and made his way slowly back to reclaim his inheritance. On the journey home he married Princess Sybil, daughter of the Count of Conversano and through her acquired a dowry, sufficient gold and silver, to buy his duchy back. Nevertheless, despite his service on behalf of the Cross, Robert seemed more desirous to go to bed than to war, so men held their breath and wondered what would truly happen. Prince Henry meanwhile, chastened by his earlier defeats, stayed close to his brother the King as he was a landowner possessing manors in Normandy and England. At the time Henry was 32 years of age and could only wait and see what God would provide.

This was the situation by July the year of Our Lord 1100. Father Anselm, Archbishop of Canterbury, was in exile at Lyons because he could not accept the Red King's attempts to subject Holy Mother Church to his own will in all things. Duke Robert, having pawned Normandy for five years to carry Christ's Blessed Cross to Jerusalem, was returning home with his new bride, the Princess Sybil. Prince Henry, closed-faced and shrewd, [I write secretly in a cipher as Father Anselm has instructed me], was a bachelor knight with estates in England and Normandy. Philip I of France sheltered behind his walls in Paris guarding the Vexin much coveted by William. The Red King himself had adjourned to Brockenhurst, his hunting lodge in the New Forest, his busy brain teeming like an upturned hive. He had driven Count Helias out of Maine and was now doing business with the Duke of Aquitaine who also wished to mortgage his estates in order to pay for an army he wanted to lead to Outremer in the service of the Cross. The future Queen Mathilda, or Edith as some preferred to call her by her font name, was still housed in the convent at Wilton protected by the veil and, as some claimed, the vows of a nun. Mathilda was the daughter of Malcolm of Scotland and Margaret, the sainted granddaughter of the great Anglo-Saxon King Edmund nicknamed 'Ironside'. Mathilda had been sent for her education to her aunt at Wilton. Certain nobles had hoped for her hand, including Warrene the Earl of Surrey. Very few knew the passion which burned between her and the William's younger brother, Henry.

The Red King arrived at Brockenhurst with leading members of his council. Principal amongst these was Robert Beaumont, Count of Meulan, who enjoyed a well-deserved reputation for cunning. Meulan is described by one chronicler as: "cold and crafty", "the Achitophel of his time". The Count of Meulan was William's chief adviser, a man who detested Duke Robert because of a quarrel between them. Years earlier Meulan had demanded the custody of Brionne Castle but Robert had refused, threw Meulan into prison and gave the Castle to someone else. Meulan had never forgotten that! In the recent war against Philip, Meulan had opened his fortress to assist William to strike at Paris and make the French King even more vulnerable. Another councillor was Fitzhaimo, a staunch supporter of the Red King, Conqueror of South Wales and a lavish benefactor of Shrewsbury Abbey and St Peter's, Gloucester. Finally there was Walter Tirel, Lord of Poix, Founder of the Abbey of St Denis du Poix and the Abbey of Pierre Salincourt, a man of Bec who had married Adelicia, sister of Gilbert and Roger De Clare, great nobles of England. As his estates were strategically placed near the Vexin, Tirel had met the Red King the previous year when William had waged war against both Helias and Philip of France. William had encouraged him to join his coterie and Tirel had become the king's close friend and guest favoured at court.

Accordingly, at the end of that July 1100, all of Europe waited and watched. Would Robert go to war over Normandy? Would he win support amongst the Lords? Would William confront him or would the Red King embark on even greater conquests in France, swallowing Aquitaine and perhaps even marching on Paris? He did boast, just before his death, how he hoped to spend Christmas at Poitiers. Others wondered what Father Anselm would do. Would he remain in exile? Or would he urge his superior, the Bishop of Rome, Paschal II, to issue solemn decrees of excommunication against the Red King, casting him from his throne, inviting others to take up the sword against him? If the Red King pondered such matters he pushed them aside. August had arrived, the grease-time, when the dapple-coated, proud-antlered stag could be hunted. William loved above all things the chase; galloping hooves, fleeing stags, barking dogs, arrows whipping through the green darkness. Once he was at Brockenhurst, William could delight himself, pondering the secret thoughts of his heart before taking action. No one really knew what he intended because, on 2nd August, God and his saints intervened.

I have visited the hunting lodge at Brockenhurst: a well-fortified place protected by palisade and ditch. Inside lies the usual bothies, out-houses, stables, granaries and stores. In the centre, on a slightly raised hill, stands a two-storey mansion of stone and timber: the upper chamber housing the hall and most of the royal apartments: the lower, the guard room and guest chambers. The King had moved there with Robert of Meulan, Fitzhaimo, Walter Tirel and others. The hunting season had begun and William was eager for fast and furious sport. On the night of 1st August, he sheltered there and seemed unaware of the rumours and dangers seething around him. Throughout the Kingdom portents and omens were seen. Something terrible was about to happen. God's vengeance was about to be carried out. Abbot Fulchered's words rang out like the bells of doom whilst other monks in their house at Gloucester gazed into the future and glimpsed the dark shapes of impending disaster.

In London packs of wild dogs suddenly appeared, short in body, large in head, with powerful jaws and extremely fierce. These animals would gather at night round St Paul's Cathedral, a great danger to man and beast as they would drag down anyone vulnerable or infirm, alone or without a weapon. Three times the citizens complained about this at the folk-moot at St Paul's Cross. The City Fathers issued an edict demanding that all dogs be locked up at night but still these ferocious packs prowled the city. At last it was decided that on a certain day all the dogs should be killed. However on the night before, the dogs, four thousand in number, fierce and snarling, abruptly disappeared. No one knew why they had gone or what had happened to them. Similar portents were reported throughout the countryside as well as in towns and villages.

Other omens were more direct. According to the Chronicle of the Abbey of St Peter's at Gloucester, a monk of good reputation and even better life, described a vision he had experienced. "I saw," he declared, "the Lord Jesus on his throne in heaven surrounded by the glorious celestial army and the choir of the saints. While I stared dumbfounded, lifted out of myself through ecstasy and in great amazement, I fixed my eyes on these marvels. I then noticed a shining virgin who entered the Lord's presence and threw herself at the feet of Jesus and implored him humbly with these prayers:

> 'Lord Jesus Christ, Saviour of man for whom you hung on the Cross and poured out your precious blood. Look with pity on your wretched people groaning under King William's yoke. Avenger of crimes! Most just of judges, take vengeance on William for my sake, rescue me from his hands, for he does all in his power to defile and oppress me brutally.'

To her the Lord replied:

> 'In patience, wait a little while, suffer a little longer but do not despair, you will soon be avenged of him.'"

Hearing these words, the monk reported, he trembled. He was certain that, at that moment, Divine wrath threatened the King. He recognised the lament as that of the Holy Virgin, our Mother the English Church whose cries had reached the ears of the Lord. Her laments concerned the plundering and shameful adulteries, the intolerable burden of evils deeds by which the Red King and his followers daily transgressed and violated God's law. The monk told his superior Abbot Serlo about what he had dreamt. The Abbot became so concerned, he immediately sat down and wrote a warning, sending it to the King at Brockenhurst, providing a lucid account of what the monk had learnt in his vision.

"On the morning of 2nd August", so this Chronicle continued, "King William was sitting at meet with his friends making preparations to go hunting in the New Forest after dinner.

He was laughing and joking with his retainers. He was putting on his boots, when a smith arrived and offered him six arrows. The Red King took these eagerly. He praised the maker for his work and, ignorant of what was about to happen, kept four for himself and handed two to Walter Tirel.

'It is only right,' the Red King remarked, 'that the keenest arrow should be given to the man who knows how to loose the deadliest shots.'

Now Tirel was a northern knight from France, a wealthy chatelain from Poix and Pontoise, a powerful magnate, a man highly skilled in the use of arms. Consequently he was one of the King's closest friend and his constant companion everywhere. "Afterwards", this Chronicle continues, "while they were discussing various critical matters, and the household retainers clustered round William, a monk from Gloucester arrived and handed Abbot Serlo's letter to the King. This was read out and, on hearing the message, the King exploded with mirth and laughingly turned to Tirel. 'Walter, do what is right in the business you have heard.' To which he replied, 'So I will, my Lord.'"

The Chronicle does not add what Tirel and the King were talking about. "However, the King was now insistent on hunting. He scorned the warnings of his betters, forgetting that pride comes before a fall. Indeed he openly criticised the contents of the letter to which he had just listened.

'I truly wonder,' the King declared, 'what has persuaded my good Abbot Serlo to tell me such things. I believe he is really a good abbot, a truly sensible man, yet he is so naïve! He insists on telling me, when I have so much real business to attend to, about the dreams of snoring monks. He even has them written down and sent across several shires to me. Does he think I act after the fashion of the English who put off their journeys and act so superstitiously, that they give up their business on account of the snores and dreams of little old women?'"

Saying this the Chronicle adds, "the King sprang to his feet, mounted his horse and galloped into the woods. His brother, Prince Henry, and other eminent men followed. They entered the wood and sent the huntsmen off to different places, as was customary. The King and Walter Tirel were standing in a glade with a few companions. As they stood on the alert, waiting for their prey, their weapons at the ready, a deer suddenly ran between them. The King drew back from his place and Walter let fly an arrow. It sped swiftly over the beast's back grazing its hide and mortally wounded the King who was standing directly in its path. He fell to the ground and died at once. When this mortal prince perished, many were thrown into great confusion. Terrible shouts that the King was dead echoed through the wood. Henry galloped at top speed to Winchester Castle where the Royal Treasure was stored, and imperiously demanded the keys from its keepers as the lawful heir. William de Breteuil, the Treasurer, also hastened there and, foreseeing Henry's design, raised objection to it.

'We ought to remember the loyalty we have promised to your brother, Duke Robert', the keeper declared. 'He is the elder son of the Great Conqueror. Both you and I, my Lord Henry, have done homage to him, which forces us to be faithful to him in everything whether he is present or not. He has toiled for years in the service of God and now God restores to him, without the strife of battle, both his Duchy which he left as a Crusader for Christ's sake, as well as his father's Crown.'

Such words led to a fierce exchange, a sharp quarrel began and a crowd of men gathered from all sides. Henry impetuously placed his hand on his sword hilt and drew the blade declaring that he would suffer no upstart causing him such ill-founded delay in seizing hold of his father's sceptre. A bloody affray was imminent. However, friends and wise councillors converged from all sides and the disturbance was quelled. More prudent advice prevailed to prevent a worst division, and the castle with its royal treasury, was handed over to Prince Henry. This, according to the Chronicle I studied, "had been prophesied long before by the magician Merlin – that the English would choose to have as their Lord, one nobly born within their own Kingdom – namely Prince Henry."

The moment the Red King was dead however, many nobles made off from the woodland to their estates and prepared to resist the orders they anticipated." The Chronicle then describes: "how humbler attendants covered the King's body as best they might with wretched cloths and carried him like a wild boar, stuck with spears, on a cart to Winchester. Clergy, monks, widows and beggars came out to meet it, as well as others of noble dignity. They quickly buried the corpse in the old Minster of St Peter. However, the churchmen present considered the Red King's squalid life and horrid death ventured past all judgement. They declared he was unworthy of absolution by the Church, since as long as he'd lived they'd never been able to turn him from his evil ways. Church bells, often sounded for the meanest kind, were not tolled for him. The huge treasure store, where many heaps of coins had been wrung from the poor, provided no alms for the needy to pray for the soul of the miserable King who'd once possessed it. However, those mercenaries, lechers and common harlots who'd lost their wages because of the death of their dissolute King, lamented his wretched end, not through any respect but from their own vile greed which fed on his vices. Indeed they searched desperately for Walter Tirel to rend him limb from limb for the death of their protector. However, as soon as the deed was done, Tirel hurried to the coast, crossed the sea and made for his castles in France where he sheltered in safety against the threats and curses of those who might wish to harm him …"

I studied this account most closely and wondered what my master would make of it but then passed on to others. Some Chroniclers were very terse. One simply declared: "On the morning after Lammas, King William was killed by an arrow while hunting, by one of his men." Another account reports: "At the time of the King's death, there were fountains flowing blood, mighty earthquakes, while the sea overflowing its shores, brought terrible afflictions to the maritime places. Murder and seditions occurred. Satan himself was seen appearing in the middle of many woods. The most shocking famine and pestilence raged amongst men as well as beasts of burden. Agriculture was almost totally neglected, as well as all care of the living or burial of the dead. The end and termination of so many woes was the death of the Red King. Now there had come from Normandy to visit the Red King, a very powerful baron, Walter Tirel by name. King William received him with the most lavish hospitality and, having honoured him with a seat at his table, was pleased after the banquet had concluded, to give him an invitation to join him in the hunt. Accordingly, they all left the hunting-lodge. Once the King had pointed out to each person his position, the deer, alarmed by the barking of the dogs and cries of the huntsmen, were sent swiftly flying towards the summit of the hill. The said Walter incautiously aimed an arrow at a stag: this missed, and pierced the King in his chest. The King fell to the earth and instantly died. Upon which, the corpse being laid by a few huntsman on a cart, was carried back to the palace. The following day it was buried with few manifestations of grief in a humble tomb. The reason for this was that all his retainers were busy attending to Prince Henry's interests and few, or none, cared for the royal funeral. Walter Tirel, the unwitting author of the King's death, escaped from the midst of them, crossed the sea and arrived safely home in Normandy ..."

Another Chronicle from Malmesbury in Wiltshire provided a full and precise account of the portents which occurred beforehand as well as after the Red King's death. I was surprised because it made reference to Father Anselm as well as a warning delivered to him about Rufus which he had never shared with me. The narrative goes as follows: "There were many different events but the most dreadful incident was that Satan visibly appeared to men in woods and secret places. Moreover, at Fitchamsted in Berkshire, a well flowed so liberally with blood for 15 whole days that it discoloured and tainted a neighbouring pool. The news was brought to King William. He laughed. He did not heed his own dreams or take notice of anything others saw concerning him. Many visions," the Chronicle continued, "had been seen prophesying his death and were vouched for by the testimony of credible witnesses. Even Father Anselm, exiled in France, had come to Lyons that he might communicate his sufferings at the hands of the English King to Hugh Abbot of Cluny. Whilst he was there the conversation turned to the Red King and Abbot Hugh declared:

'Last night William of England was brought before God's tribunal, judgement was incurred and the terrible sentence of damnation imposed.'

How he came to know this was not explained at the time …" I paused and tapped the manuscript. I wondered if that were true and why my master had not told me? I returned to the Chronicle.

"The day before the King died, he dreamed he was being bled by a surgeon and the gush of blood streamed to heaven clouding the skies and obscuring the day. Calling to Our Lady for protection, the Red King abruptly awoke and told his attendants not to leave him, but that candles be lit and lanterns fired. Shortly afterwards, just before daybreak, a certain foreign monk came to Fitzhaimo, one of the chief noblemen at the court, and told him about a dreadful dream he had about the King.

'The King', he declared, 'swaggered into our church with certain threats and boasts as was his custom. He looked arrogantly about at his friends then, seizing a crucifix, gnawed the arms and almost tore away the legs. The image suffered this for a while, but at last struck the King with its foot so he fell backwards and from his mouth belched such flame and smoke it touched the very stars.' Lord Fitzhaimo, thinking this should not be ignored, went to the King with whom he was very intimate. Once he'd heard this, the King burst into raucous laughter and said:

'Fitzhaimo, he's a monk and dreams for money, give him a

100 shillings.'

Nonetheless, the Red King was not unmoved. Because of his own dreams and those of others told to him, he hesitated a long time about whether he should go hunting or not, his friends urging him not to take the risk of testing the truth of all these portents. Accordingly he did not hunt before dinner but tended to serious business, thereby keeping himself busy, and thus dispelling his uneasiness. He soothed his cares with more wine and food than usual, then after dinner went into the forest with a very small number of attendants. Amongst these, the most intimate with Rufus was Walter Tirel who'd come from France, attracted by the liberality of the King. This man remained alone with him whilst others were scattered wildly in the chase. The sun was now setting. The King drew his bow and let fly an arrow which slightly wounded a stag which passed before him. He ran in pursuit, keeping his gaze fixed rigidly on his quarry and raised up his hand to shield his eyes from the sun's rays. Walter tried to hit another stag, which by chance came near him, while the King's attention was otherwise occupied. So, unknowingly, without the power to prevent it, [Oh Gracious God!], he pierced the King's breast with a fatal arrow. When William received the wound he said not a word but, breaking the shaft, fell to the ground and thus brought about his own death more speedily. Walter immediately ran up, but finding the King senseless and speechless, he leapt quickly on his horse and escaped at full gallop. Indeed there were none to pursue him. Some connived at his flight, others ignored him, everybody was intent on other matters. A few rustics took care of the royal corpse, put it on a cart and took it to the cathedral at Winchester, the blood dripping from it all the way. Here he was committed to the ground beneath the tower, attended by many of his minions, but mourned by few others."

Another Chronicle provides the same details but harked back to earlier deaths of William's family, in particular Prince Richard, William's elder brother, as well as the King's bastard nephew also called Richard, who were both killed while hunting in the New Forest. It reads as follows: "On Thursday 2nd August, at the eighth hour, William the Younger, King of England, while engaged hunting in the New Forest which in the land of the English is called Ytienne (or the land of the Jutes), was struck by an arrow carelessly aimed by a certain henchman, Walter Tirel, and died. He was brought to Winchester and buried in the Old Minster church of St Peter. No wonder," as the Chronicle confirms, "that God's power and anger were shown, because in the olden times during Edward the Confessor's reign and those of other Kings who were his predecessors, the region abounded in churches and worshippers of God, but at the bidding of King William the Conqueror, men were driven away, their houses burned down, their churches destroyed and the land made only fit for wild animals. This, it is believed, was the cause of great misfortune. The Red King's elder brother, Richard, perished in the same forest, shot by an arrow by one of his knights while he himself was hunting. A similar fate befell another Richard, the bastard son of William's brother, Duke Robert. The forest was truly cursed. In the place where the Red King fell a church once stood but during his father's reign this had been cruelly destroyed."

This story was repeated time and again in the Chronicle accounts provided. I noticed how Father Anselm had sent Ivo and Reginald not only to English houses but also to those across the Narrow Seas: the priories and monasteries of Normandy. Each had a different perspective or slant to this story, in the end I formed them into one coherent whole, though I was still not able to judge what was true or not.

I left the Chronicle versions and asked the librarian for any charts or maps of the area. Apparently the Red King had stayed at his lodge at Brockenhurst, but the hunt actually rode south-west towards Througham where the incident took place. Once there, the King went down from his horse so as to take better aim, Tirel and the other Lords also dismounted. Walter apparently placed himself near an elder tree behind an aspen. A great stag passed by and an arrow, badly aimed by Tirel, pierced the King. Walter froze with fright. The King fell. He called for God's body, the consolamentum, the Eucharist, but there was none there to give it to him. The place was a wilderness far from any church so one of the hunters took herbs and flowers and made the dying King eat, deeming this to be communion.

In another description of Rufus' death, the King had frightful dreams which were interpreted by a holy Bishop (I rejected this as more wishful thinking than the truth). However, according to this version, the King, his companions and servants made ready for the hunt. They mount their horses, the bows are ready, the dogs are leashed, the horns blow. The Red King is still unwilling to leave. His companions tempt him to hunt and jeer at him when he declines. He tells them solemnly that he is sick at heart and very sad, the end is nigh, he will not go into the forest. They think that he is mocking them and at last persuade him to come. The chase is described. The King apparently becomes separated from the rest except for one companion. William calls on this comrade to shoot, but he is unwilling, being too near the King. At last he looses and the devil guides the barbed arrow so it glances off a tree and pierces the King in the heart. William collapses. He has just enough strength to bid the knight to flee for his own life. He prays to God for himself who'd lost his life by his own stupidity as he had been a great sinner against God. The knight rides off in bitter grief wishing a hundred times that he himself had been killed rather than the King.

In another narrative the actual stag came between Tirel and the King. Walter looses at the same time as the Red King shifts his place. Tirel's arrow flies over the stag's back and pierces the King. One particular Chronicle emphasises how the King was pierced, but made matters worst by stumbling and falling on the arrow, driving the barb deeper into his chest. In a separate account, the string of the King's bow broke, the stag stopped, possibly frightened, and the King called out to Tirel, "Shoot you devil! Shoot in the devil's name! Shoot, or it will be the worse for you!" Walter loosed his arrow, it glanced off a tree, striking the King in the heart.

In most of the accounts, the King was either alone or those with him fled, leaving his corpse to the care of common retainers. Only in one version did the lords gather round the corpse, leading men of the royal council, including Fitzhaimo. These lords weep. They wish they were dead and loudly mourn the loss of such a good Seigneur. Eventually, one of them tells the rest to stop lamenting and pay honours to what was left of their Lord. Huntsmen are summoned, they fashion a bier, strew it with flowers and fasten it between two palfries. They place the corpse on the bier, cover it with Fitzhaimo's mantle and take it sorrowfully to Winchester for burial. This rendition certainly contradicted the accepted version of many Chronicles where only a few peasants from the neighbourhood look after the Red King's remains. Accordingly I regarded such a tale as very fanciful.

I then turned to what happened after William's death and came across yet another story which involved my master. On 1st August, 1100 a young man glowing with light stood before Anselm's doorkeeper at Lyons as he tried to sleep. This luminous young man asked if my master had heard the news that the strife between King William and Archbishop Anselm was over? The fellow replied that he hadn't. The next day, when the Red King actually died, one of the archbishop's clerks singing in the choir with his eyes shut, felt a small piece of parchment pushed into his hand and a voice whispered at him to read. He looked up, but the bearer of the message was gone so he read the words "King William is dead." Jesu Miserere! I sat and stared at the window. I could not recall such an incident! Did it happen? Had my master kept it confidential from me?

Two other stories attracted my attention. At the same hour that the Red King went out into the New Forest, his cousin,

William of Mortaine, was also hunting in Cornwall. He, too, found himself alone on the very evening his royal cousin was killed and saw a frightful apparition. A huge goat with black, shaggy coat met him, bearing on his back the Red King, now naked and wounded in the chest. Mortaine, in the name of Christ, ordered the beast to stop and say what it all meant? The goat replied: "I bear your King, or rather your tyrant, William the Red, to his eternal doom, for I am an evil spirit. I am the avenger of the wickedness which this King waged against the Church of Christ. I have brought about his death at the bidding of those who made their groans to the Lord because this man sinned beyond all measure."

The second tale concerned the King's younger brother Prince Henry. He was hunting in the New Forest but not in the immediate vicinity of his royal brother. According to this story, the string of Henry's bow also broke, so he went to a charcoal burner's house to have it mended. Whilst this was happening an old woman asked one of the Prince's companions who his master was? He replied that he was Henry, brother of the King. She replied that she knew from the signs that the King's brother would soon be King himself and told him to remember her words. Henry's bow was mended and he returned to the hunt only to be met by individuals, followed by others, carrying dreadful news. In his grief Henry went to the place where his brother's corpse lay and then rode swiftly to Winchester …

II

Lauds

Historical Notes

The main secondary sources for the reign of William Rufus are: Frank Barlow, *William Rufus* (Methuen, 1983); Arthur Lloyd, *The Death of Rufus* (New Forest Museum, 2000); E.A Freeman, *The Reign of William Rufus* (1882), Vols. I-II; D. Grinnell Milne, *The Killing of William Rufus* (1968). The latter concentrates on Rufus' death in a most bewildering manner – trying to recreate topography, climate – even the movements of deer over six hundred years earlier! Lloyd's book is very scholarly and pertinent: he presents the facts but believes Rufus' death was an accident, as does Barlow. Indeed this seems to be the line taken by most historians except for Milne; such theories will be discussed later. Rufus' reputation was undoubtedly demonised by monastic chroniclers bitterly opposed to him. E.A. Freeman was also very condemnatory. Barlow tones this down, emphasizing Rufus' strength as a king, his skill as a general and his bravery as a warrior. Rufus' sexual life is difficult to determine, there are dark hints about homosexuality and of prostitutes of either sex being favoured at his court. William was a blunt, fearsome character turned into an ogre by many chroniclers, a matter taken up by T. Callahan Jr. in his article 'The Making of a Monster: the historical image of William Rufus', *Journal of Mediaeval History*, VII,

(1981), p.175 and E. Mason, 'William Rufus: myth and reality', *Journal of Mediaeval History*, III (1977). D.C. Douglas, *William the Conqueror* (1964) is still the best analysis of the Great Conqueror, his family and his policies, especially that of afforestation. The development and extension of the New Forest is still a matter for debate but no one denies the influence of the Norman Kings in the protection and enhancement of these hunting preserves. See also O. Rackham, *Ancient Woodland* (1980). On the villainous Ranulf Flambard, Oderic Vitalis and Simeon of Durham *Historical Works* (*Historia Ecclesial Dunelmensis*) I, (Rolls Series, 1882), ed. T. Arnold. On Gerard and the Pig and other associated scandals: Hugh Flavigny's *Chronicon*, ed. G.H. Petry in *Monumenta Germaniae Historiarum Scriptores*, Vol. VIII, pp.495-97.

The Chronicle accounts for the Red King's death are fairly extensive but many simply repeat the accepted story. Of course, some of these accounts were written much later but they represent what was known in a certain area, very much like today when one provincial newspaper may take a 'slant' on a national event that is totally different from that adopted by another. The Chronicles are as follows:

The Anglo Saxon Chronicle bluntly states how William was killed by one of his men in that year (1100), (Rolls Series, 1861) II, p.203.

Eadmer, *Historia Novorum in Anglia*, simply declares the King was killed.

Peter of Blois (c.1068-1118): *Rerum Anglicorum Scriptores*, ed. Gale (1684), I, pp.10-11, maintains that the King's death, though shadowed by portents like the apparition of the devil, was an accident. Tirel was the King's special guest; he missed a stag, hit the King then fled. The royal corpse was then loaded onto a cart and taken to Winchester.

William of Malmesbury (c.1095-1143) drew on several accounts in his *De Gestis Rerum Anglicorum*, ed. W. Stubbs, (Rolls

Series, 1887-1889), Vol. II, pp.377-79. He mentions the dreams and portents. How the Red King soothed his ill-humours on 2nd August with food and drink. Tirel is depicted as a boon-companion of the King. He goes hunting with him, misses his target and hits the King, who is staring in the direction of the setting sun, shading his eyes. The stricken King breaks off the shaft but falls on the barb. Tirel flees, "some conniving at his flight". William's corpse, "the blood dripping from it all along the way", is taken by "rustici" (country people) to Winchester.

Oderic Vitalis (op. cit.) pp.284-85, mentions the other two royal deaths in the New Forest, (Richard and Richard), the clearing of the forest as a royal hunting preserve, the gift of the six arrows and the Red King giving two of these to Tirel. Oderic also informs us of the following: Abbot Serlo's letter; William's mockery of it as well as the Red King's charge to Tirel which, in one translation, can be, "Walter, do what is just (right) in the matters (business) you've heard". Oderic maintains that Tirel accidentally loosed an arrow, it skimmed the animal and hit the King. Oderic describes Rufus' sudden death, the consternation it caused, the hasty departure for Winchester, the confrontation there between Prince Henry and others and the swift, low-key burial of the dead King, (op. cit.), pp.291-95.

Matthew Paris (c.1250) in his *Chronica Major*, ed. H.R. Luard (Rolls Series, 1874), Vol. II, pp.111-12, talks of the arrow ricocheting from a tree and hitting the King.

Geoffrey Gaimar, *Lestoire des Engles*, ed. T. Hardy and C. Martin (Rolls Series, 1889), provides the detailed description, [Section III, lines 6311-21] of the Red King's nobles gathering mournfully around the royal corpse.

Henry Knighton, writing much later, *Chronica Henrici Knighton*, ed. J.R. Lumby (Rolls Series, 1889), Vol. II, gives the story about the King's bowstring being broken and the shouting which occurred ("Loose you devil or it will be the worse for you"). An interesting story coming from the area where de Beaumont's influence (Robert of Meulan and Henry of Warwick) was very strong.

All the above accounts describe William's impetuous character – for example the mad dash across the channel to save the city of Le Mans (Eadmer, *Historia Novorum*, pp.166- 67). The story of William of Mortain's vision is found in Matthew Paris' *Historia Anglicana*, ed. J.R. Luard, Vol. I, p.71. The story about Prince Henry's bowstring being broken is to be found in a much later Chronicle, Wace's *Le Roman de Rou de Wace*, ed. A.J. Holden (Paris 1971). The mysterious messengers/envoys who come to Cluny to advise Anselm of the Red King's death are actually from Eadmer's *Life of Anselm*, ed. R.W. Southern (1962), pp.122-24. However, in his *Historia Novorum*, Eadmer does not mention such startling prodigies – the truth being that Eadmer's history was strictly scholarly whilst the *Vita Sancti Anselmi*, in the fashion of the times, is hagiography. On Tirel himself and his background, the best study is J.H. Round's *Feudal England* (New ed. 1964), p.355 et seq., which depicts Tirel as an important French magnate, a great friend of the Benedictines, certainly at least an acquaintance of Anselm with strong ties to Anselm's Monastery at Bec. At this point in the narrative I do not wish to engage in proof or counter-proof except to note that Eadmer stood at the heart of royal power in England: he was secretary to Anselm, he had access to people and records yet he never actually states that Tirel was the killer of the Red King.

III

Prime

The Bows of the Mighty are broken.
(I. Samuel 2)

I finished my compendium of Chronicle accounts about the Red King's death. I then immediately drew up a clear description of events, from those same narratives, which occurred during the two years following the Red King's death. It reads as follows:
"In the year of our Lord 1100, on Thursday 2nd August, William Rufus was killed by an arrow in the New Forest after ruling England for 12 years and almost ten months. Henry, his brother, hurried to London with Robert, Count of Meulan, and on the following Sunday, he received the Royal Crown in the church of St Peter the Apostle at Westminster. Maurice, the Bishop of London, consecrated him. Anselm, Archbishop of Canterbury, was still in exile, whilst Thomas, Archbishop of York, had recently died, so that the Metropolitan See was still vacant. Henry was over 30 years old when he began to reign. He governed the realm committed to him by God, prudently and well, through prosperity and adversity. Among all the distinguished rulers of Christendom, he is considered outstanding for his preservation of peace and justice. At the beginning of his reign, the Church of God enjoyed riches and honours, and every religious order began to flourish to the glory of God. Monks and clerks bear witness to this, for they increased in number and distinction once Henry became King."

[I thought I was being overly flattering but, from the accounts I studied, the relief of churchmen at the Red King's death and Henry's accession was palpable].

"At the beginning of his reign the new King wisely recommended himself to all men, inviting them into his favour with royal gifts. He treated the magnates with honour and generosity, adding to their wealth and estates and, by treating them in this way, won their loyalty. He helped his humbler subjects by giving just laws, and protected them by his patronage from unjust extortions and robbers." [I must concede King Henry promised a great deal, everything to everyone, including my master. Henry created the illusion of harmony, but for many, though not for Anselm, that was enough].

"When Hugh, Earl of Chester, Robert of Bellême and other magnates who were in Normandy, heard of the death of the Red King and the sudden revolution which followed, they settled their affairs in Normandy and hurried back to England. They dutifully submitted to the new King and, after performing homage, received their estates and all their dignities from him, together with royal gifts. King Henry did not follow the advice of rash young men, but prudently took to heart the experience and advice of wiser and older men. He invited into his secret chamber Robert of Meulan, Fitzhaimo and Henry of Warwick.

In the fourth month of his reign Henry, not wishing to wallow in hot lechery like any sparrow which is without the use of reason, married in royal state, the royal maiden named Mathilda, and had by her two children, Mathilda and William. Henry's Queen was the daughter of Malcolm, King of Scots, and Queen Margaret, who was descended from the stock of King Alfred, son of King Egbert, the line which first ruled all England after the Danish war until the murder of St Edmund, King and martyr. So Henry in his wisdom, appreciating the high birth of the maiden whose perfection of character he had long adored, chose her as his bride in Christ and raised her to the throne beside himself.

In the month of August 1100 however, as soon as the unfortunate death of the Red King was proclaimed in Normandy, the passions of the unruly Normans spilled out into civil war. That very same week, Norman lords invaded the Beaumont lands with a strong force and seized considerable booty from the land of Robert, Count of Meulan, in revenge for injuries that he had done to his peers for some time past, by turning Rufus against them through false allegations. Many others, who had been nursing anger and hatred, also participated in this violence. Previously they had not dared to avenge themselves openly because of the strict justice maintained by the Red King. They now fell upon each other without restraint once he was dead, and by their mutual slaughter and pillaging, devastated Normandy.

In September, Duke Robert arrived in Normandy and, after being received by his people, went with his wife Sibyl to Mont St Michel. There he gave thanks to God for his safe return from his long pilgrimage and his marriage to the daughter of Geoffrey of Conversano. In the New Year, she bore him a son, and Archbishop William baptized the child, giving him his own name. Duke Robert recovered his duchy without opposition. However, he held it for about eight years in name only as he was sunk beyond redemption in indolence and voluptuousness, which made him an object of contempt to the restless and lawless Normans. Theft and rapine were daily occurrences, and brutalities increased everywhere, to the ruin of the entire province.

"In September, the year of our Lord, 1101, a great revolt broke out in England and Normandy. Turbulent magnates, alarmed by the energy of King Henry, and preferring the mildness of the sluggard Duke Robert, who left them freer to pursue their evil ambitions, began to organise treacherous conventicles with one another. These advised Duke Robert to prepare a fleet and cross the Narrow Seas at the earliest opportunity. Robert of Bellème and William of Warenne, Earl of Surrey, as well as many others, approved the plotted revolt and helped the adherents of the Duke, secretly at first, and then openly. The reckless Duke agreed with them. He did not give good government to his own dominions, but foolishly neglected them out of greed for the Kingdom which his abler brother possessed.

The Norman magnates, who regarded Duke Robert with contempt and were more ready to follow the English King, resolved to offer the Duchy of Normandy to Henry and sent messenger after messenger to tempt Henry to accept it. So both peoples were corrupted by the climate of treason, and plotted deeds of treachery to harm their lords. Some rebels waged open war against loyal neighbours and stained the fertile soil with ravages, conflagrations, and bloody slaughter. The venerable Archbishop Anselm and all the bishop and abbots with the consecrated clergy, as well as the Saxons, preserved their unshaken loyalty to their King and offered ceaseless prayers to the Lord of Hosts for his safety and the preservation of the realm. Robert of Meulan and many other loyal and provident barons, followed their lord faithfully and supplied him with counsel and military support.

The chief instigator of this plot against King Henry was Ranulf Flambard, Bishop of Durham. Rising from low origins, Ranulf had been a sycophant of William Rufus and had so pandered to him with his cunning machinations, that the King had raised him above all the magnates of the realm. Ranulf became chief manager of the King's wealth as well as Justiciar, and through his many acts of cruelty, made himself hated and feared by most men. He himself grew wealthy with the riches he raked in from all sides and the enlargement of his estates. Indeed, in spite of being almost illiterate, Ranulf was promoted to a Bishop's Chair, not because of any piety, but through secular power. However, since no power is long enduring in this mortal life, after Rufus' death, Ranulf was imprisoned by the new King as an inveterate plunderer of the country. For the many injuries Ranulf had inflicted on Henry himself and his subjects, poor as well as rich, and the many ways in which he had often impiously oppressed the suffering, God intervened. When the wind of fortune changed, Ranulf was hurled from the summit of power to be imprisoned in chains in the White Tower near London. Truly, as Ovid says in his poem about Daedalus: "Often misfortunes stir the wits."

The ingenious bishop plotted to escape from such close imprisonment and craftily arranged his flight through friends. Ranulf was resourceful and persuasive and, though cruel and quick-tempered, he was also generous and affable on many occasions, so that numerous people found him agreeable and likeable. He received by the King's command, two shillings sterling for food every day. Using this as well as the help of his friends, Ranulf made merry in prison and every day ordered a fine feast to be set before him and his guards. One day a rope was smuggled to him in a flagon of wine, whilst plentiful provisions for the feast were purchased by the Bishop's largesse. The guards feasted with him and grew merry as they drained copious draughts of Falernian wine. When they were thoroughly drunk and safely snoring, the bishop fastened the rope to a mullion in the middle of a window in the tower and, taking his pastoral staff with him, slid down the rope. However, as he had forgotten to protect his hands with gloves, they were torn to the bone by the roughness of the rope and, as it did not reach quite down to the ground, the portly ecclesiastic suffered a heavy fall which almost flattened him. [It certainly made him scream with pain]. However his loyal friends had good horses ready for him. Mounting, he fled like the wind, being met on his way by trusted companions who brought him treasure. Accompanied by them, Ranulf sailed swiftly towards Normandy to find Duke Robert.

Ranulf Flambard's mother, who was a sorceress and had often conversed with the devil, [in fact she had lost an eye through this infamous familiarity], was also conveyed across the sea to Normandy in another ship with her son's treasure. She was highly unpleasant to the crew so her companions in the boat mocked her with crude gestures for her accursed incantations. In the course of the voyage pirates attacked this ship and plundered all the treasure. Flambard's old witch of a mother was deposited, naked and sorrowing, along with the rest of the crew and guards on the Normandy shore.

Ranulf Flambard was more fortunate. The fugitive Bishop was given refuge by Duke Robert and appointed to a position of authority in Normandy. The Duke himself profited from Ranulf's counsels, as far as his indolence allowed. Flambard especially urged the duke to a trial of strength with his brother Henry and stirred up hostility against the King by every means in his powers. He advised the duke on how he might best secure the Kingdom of England and promised his help in all that he did.

At length, Duke Robert sailed to England. After being received as King by the distinguished and wealthy men who had formed the conspiracy and were expecting him, Duke Robert prepared for war. The Duke quickly established himself in the district round Winchester, where he was joined by certain nobles of the realm who paid homage to him. Urged on by such rebels, Robert challenged his brother to meet him in battle unless he was prepared to renounce the crown. Many who had formerly made a show of supporting the King were eager to welcome the Duke when he arrived and so swelled his army with their forces. William, Earl of Surrey, and many more deserted the King. Numerous others made unreasonable demands in order to invent pretexts for breaking away, threatening to leave him unless he granted their petitions. On the other hand, Robert of Meulan, Fitzhaimo, Henry of Warwick and many other able barons protected their King, as did the Saxons, who did not recognise the rights of Duke Robert. They persisted in their loyalty to their King and were ready to go to battle to prove it.

When the Count of Meulan, who was determined to protect his own loyalty to his friend, the King, through thick and thin, saw the foul betrayals of his fellow nobles, he quietly turned many matters over in his mind and prudently worked for the safety of the realm. With this aim he said to the King, 'Every noble man who has aspired to knighthood and sees his friend hard pressed in the battle must, if he wants to be considered worthy of his calling, go to the aid of that friend in his hour of need. In such a situation one does not think about future reward but of rescuing a friend in peril. Now indeed, we see many behaving in a very different fashion, and staining with heinous treason the true faith they have pledged to their Lord. Such things are clear for us to see and we feel such sharp betrayals in our hearts. We therefore have been entrusted by God to provide for the common good. We must keep a sharp guard to preserve both the safety of this realm and the peace of Holy Mother Church. Let our chief concern be to triumph peacefully by God's grace and win a victory without shedding Christian blood, so that our loyal people may enjoy the security of peace. Now hear my advice, my lord King, and do not scorn to follow my counsel. Speak to all your knights with tact: coax them as a father would his sons, placate every one with promises, grant whatever they ask, and in this fashion draw all men assiduously to your cause. If they ask for London or York, do not hesitate to promise great rewards appropriate to kingly generosity. It is better to cede a small part of your Kingdom than to sacrifice victory and life itself to a host of enemies. When, with God's help, we come safely to the end of this danger, we shall propose practical measures for recovering the lands appropriated by rash deserters in a time of war. Indeed, anyone who chooses to desert his King in an hour of deadly danger and seek another lord for greedy gain, or insists on payment for military service which he should offer freely to his King for the defence of the realm, and attempts to deprive him of his own estates, will be judged a traitor by a just and equitable judgement. Such a traitor will rightly be deprived of his inheritance and forced to flee this Kingdom.'

All the Lords who were with King Henry applauded the Count's speech and urged the King to follow his advice. Being a

Prince of deep wisdom, Henry thanked the councillors who wished him well and eagerly accepted their pragmatic suggestions, winning with promises and gifts the support of many whom he regarded with deep suspicion. Then he went to meet his brother with a huge army and despatched messengers ahead to discover why Duke Robert had dared to enter the Kingdom with an armed force. Duke Robert replied through his own envoys, 'I have entered the realm of our father with my lords as I demand the rights due to me as his eldest son.'

The two brothers remained for some days encamped in a certain spot, noble envoys going to and fro. The treacherous rebels hoped for war rather than peace and, because they were more concerned with their selfish interests than the common good, cunning messengers twisted words and sowed seeds of dispute rather than harmony between the brothers. However, the prudent Henry realized this, and demanded to speak to his brother face to face. When they met, feelings of brotherly love surged between them both. The huge army encircled them with men of noble rank, and the appearance of both Normans and English in arms was fair yet fearful. The two brothers talked alone in the midst of the circle of onlookers, and openly and honestly voiced what they hid in their hearts. Finally, after a few words, they embraced one another and, exchanging the kiss of peace, were reconciled without any mediation.

First, Duke Robert renounced in favour of his brother the claim he had made to the Kingdom of England, and, out of respect for his royal dignity, released him from the homage which he had previously done him. In return, King Henry promised to pay the Duke 3000 pounds sterling every year. He also ceded to Robert the County of Cotentin and everything else he possessed in Normandy. Henry only retained for himself the stronghold of Domfront because he had given a sworn pledge to the men there when they'd opened their gates to him, that he would never allow them to pass out of his own land, or change their laws and customs.

Since no mediators were present, the brothers alone confirmed their undertakings and determined, while all around looked on with wonder, that they would assist one another as brothers should. They accepted the teaching of the Book of Proverbs: 'Brothers united are as a fortress'. They also agreed to recover all the domains of their father and punish on both sides the wicked men who had nourished discord between them.

Peace was made and the traitors covered in confusion. They had become hateful even to those on whom they had fawned deceitfully, so they were forced to hide ingloriously from the King's sight, trembling with fear. The honest folk and all who went about their lawful business were happy. The forces were disbanded by the King's command and returned home rejoicing. England basked in the glow of peace whilst the Church of God, enjoying a long period of calm, served God unmolested by the clash of battle.

After Duke Robert had remained for two months with his brother, the King, he returned to Normandy, laden with royal gifts. He took with him William of Warenne and many others who had been disinherited in his cause …"

I stopped. I had written the account for my master in the usual voice of the Chronicles so what more was there to say? By 1102 Henry was victorious, though it took another four years to settle the rebels in Normandy by his victory at Tinchebrai where at last he brought all his opponents to battle, defeated them, took his brother Robert prisoner and annexed Normandy to the English crown.

III

Prime
Historical Notes

The best accounts of the crises of 1100-1102 and 1105-1106 can be found in R.W. Southern, *Anselm and his Biographer* (Oxford, 1963), p.163 et seq.; E.A. Freeman (op. cit.), Vol. 2, p.343 et seq. and Sally N. Vaughan's *Anselm of Bec and Robert of Meulan* (1987), p.214 et seq. The account given here is accurate but, like many Chronicles, tends to 'enhance' Henry's reputation. However, to me, Henry was truly sinister. I agree with Southern's assessment (op. cit): "Despite the more favourable opinion of his contemporaries Henry's personality makes a more unpleasing impression than that of Rufus. He was equally licentious and avaricious." A contemporary, Robert de Bloet, Bishop of Lincoln, in his *De Contemptu Mundi* placed his finger on Henry's nefarious duplicity: "when he was praising anyone, he was sure to be plotting that person's destruction". His brother Robert, however, was aimless and carefree and, against such an opponent as Henry, virtually powerless. Meulan's speech comes direct from the primary sources [though Henry needed little encouragement in his duplicity] and clearly illustrates that noble's wily mind. Flambard was a moving force in the revolt of 1102. His escape from the Tower was one of the most brilliantly executed. In August 1323 the same tactic was employed by Roger Mortimer: he and Flambard were two of the very few prisoners who escaped from that grim, close fortress.

IV

Terce

They sharpen their tongues like Swords
They aim bitter words like arrows.
(Psalm 63)

I finished my task in the early hours of 26th July, 1108. I then read through everything I had transcribed and studied. I kept myself locked away in that chamber, going out now and again to take the air, visit the refectory, or stand in the nave of the church listening to the good brothers chanting. Anselm never approached me until one morning after he'd celebrated his Jesus Mass, he joined me in that narrow chamber. He put his hand on my shoulder, leaned over and looked at what I was writing.

"You have been through everything, Brother Eadmer? I mean from the Red King's death to Henry's great victory?"

I glanced up at him. "Master, everything you have collected and given me, I have studied and collated."

"And?" Anselm asked.

"There are stories – " I tapped the quill against the parchment " – that you knew of Rufus' death long before you should have done."

Father Anselm narrowed his eyes. "That's legend," he whispered, "or gossip – there's little truth in it." He shrugged. "If hindsight was a virtue, we'd all be saints. I cannot remember when such stories first appeared. If they did before 2nd August of that year, then the news was never passed on to me. What is interesting

– " he held up a hand, " – is so much emphasis is laid on these legends. Why, Eadmer, was it so important that prophecies, portents, omens and visions about the Red King's death be described so plentifully before the event? I have, for years, always wondered about that!"

"Father, you never shared that with me!"

"Brother," he teased, "you never asked! Reflect Eadmer!" He leaned over my shoulder again, his lips almost touching my ear. "God does work in wondrous ways, yet have you noticed how the news of Rufus' death was spread immediately? How people knew he was going to die? Do you know, Brother, I would like to think that God was warning us all but, somehow, …" he let his words hang in the air. "You are finished?"

I nodded. Anselm stretched out his hands and I gave him the manuscript. He thumbed through the pages quickly.

"I will read this," he said, and turning, stick tapping the ground, he left the chamber.

I am the Archbishop's secretary, his chancery clerk. I am excused from the horarium and the usual burdens of monastic life, so for most of that day I rested and slept. When I did awake and go out, a lay-brother informed me that Father Anselm had returned to his usual seat in the herbarium. I found him in a flower-covered alcove going through the manuscript I had prepared. On the seat beside him was a writing tray with an ink pot, a quill-pen and a roll of parchment. I went to approach him but he held his hand up.

"Paxe et bonum, Frater," he whispered.

"Peace and good to you, Father."

"Do not disturb me now, perhaps tomorrow." Anselm tapped the manuscript. "I've learnt so much, especially from your account about what happened after the Red King's death. Who was loyal, who was not. Anyway, these matters will wait."

The following morning, long before dawn, Father Anselm walked into my cell to rouse me. He stood there, cowl pulled over his head, in one hand his ave beads, in the other a lantern. He held this up and smiled.

"Do not sleep, Brother. Today is busy – come, come!"

I washed quickly at the lavarium, donned my daily robes and joined him in church. It was cold. The sun had yet to rise and only the candles in the sanctuary provided pools of glowing light. We chanted the Divine Office together then vested and celebrated the Mass of the day in chantry chapels along the north transept. Afterwards we broke our fast in the refectory on bread, honey and watered ale. Anselm insisted that we adjourn immediately to his chamber where, as he put it, he could address the business of the day.

The chamber, despite the summer, was cold. We had to wait for a lay-brother to bring in a brazier on wheels, fanning the coals, sprinkling them with herbs, stoking them so that the heat glowed out. After he had gone, Anselm wrapped a cloak about him, sat on a stool next to the desk and peered up at me.

"Write what I say, Brother – " he tapped his head, " – before I forget. If you wish you may interrupt. But first, Brother Eadmer, tell me this, as you must answer to the God you have just consumed."

"Yes, Master?"

"Having read what you have, knowing what you do now, in your judgement, do you think William the Red King was killed by accident?"

I stared at my master's face. He looked grey, tired and weary. I noticed how his hand kept touching his stomach, though his eyes were as bright and lively as they used to be when he was teaching in the schools, preaching from the pulpit or defending his cause against the King's ministers. I opened my mouth to reply.

"Don't tell me what logic dictates." Anselm moved his hand and touched his chest. "What do you feel here, Eadmer?"

"There is something very wrong," I confessed.

Anselm held my gaze and nodded. "I agree, Brother, and I am going to discover what. So, pick up your pen and let us list our information. Let us try and sift the truth from the lie, the fact from the fable."

I know my master, so saintly and good – he can also be as mischievous as an imp! I caught a twinkle in his eye, a slight lilt in his voice.

"Father Anselm?"

"Yes?"

"Have I read everything? Have you told me everything?" Anselm stared up at the ceiling, stifling a laugh.

"You haven't!" I accused putting the quill down.

"Not everything! If I had given you everything, Brother, you may have jumped to one conclusion, when I would much prefer that, as logic dictates, you reach carefully, by due process, the truth of the matter." He lifted his hands. "So, let us begin."

I dipped the quill-pen into the ink.

"Item: Let us say," Anselm declared, "for sake of argument, that the Red King was universally hated, which he certainly wasn't. In such a situation anyone could be responsible for his death: an outraged husband, brother or lover could soon learn that it was the fat season, the grease-time. The Red King loved the hunt. Brockenhurst was the preferred lair for him and his favourites. A would-be assassin could enter the forest, wait for the King to leave his hunting lodge, follow him and slay him." Anselm rested his elbows on his knees cupping his chin in his hands and glanced swiftly up at me.

"What say you, Brother?" He imitated the harsh voice of a Magister in the Schools.

"Foolish," I taunted, "and three times foolish." I added with a smile. "What motive would such a man have?"

"As I said some outraged husband ..."

"Who?"

Anselm shrugged.

"Who?" I repeated. "No evidence exists of anyone being made a cuckold by Rufus. He had his own whores and catamites. I could find no evidence of any attempted seduction of a great and noble lady. Moreover ..."

"Moreover, what?"

"That would be a dangerous way to wreak revenge. Any stranger caught armed in a royal forest was courting death. Even a clerk cannot claim benefit of clergy for violation of the Forest Laws. You must remember, Master, the woods and glades of the New Forest, particularly on such an evening, would be guarded by verderers, foresters, dog men, guards from the Royal Household, King's retainers, men who would soon recognise a stranger. In the end it was Tirel who was named – no-one else."

I am not too sure what my master whispered in reply. I thought I heard the words: "Is it now? Is it now?" I was about to question him but Anselm lifted a hand.

"So, Eadmer." My master went across to warm his vein-streaked hands over the brazier. "If it wasn't some hapless cuckold or revenge-seeker, as you say, could it have been an accident?"

"They are common enough," I replied. "Richard, son of the Conqueror was killed in the New Forest."

"By an arrow?" Anselm asked. "Or was it collision with a tree?"

"Another, Richard, the bastard son of Robert, Duke of Normandy, was also slain there."

"Again," Anselm intervened, "was he killed by an arrow or an overhanging branch? Strange, isn't it?" Anselm mused. "How in the space of what, Eadmer, 26 years, three men from the same family are killed in a similar fashion, a hunting accident in the same forest in Hampshire. Have you ever heard the like before?" He did not wait for an answer. "And why should Tirel loose a shaft so clumsily? From what I read he was a master bowman. Nor do I believe the stories about the arrow being deflected from a tree or even a roaming stag, then by sheer coincidence, piercing the King to his heart. Ah, well." Anselm grasped his stick more firmly. "Come, brother, let's see what Oderic has prepared for us." And, waggling ink-stained fingers at me, Anselm lifted his walking stick and strode vigorously to the door. He paused, hand on the latch and looked back over his shoulder.

"Well," he smiled, "aren't you coming to watch the archery?"

I climbed down from my writing stool and hastily followed him out. We hurried along the stone galleries and paved passageway, past monks scurrying here and there on some errand, tonsured-heads bowed, hands tucked up the voluminous sleeves of their gowns, sandaled feet slapping on the hardstone. When they recognised Father Anselm, they stopped and bowed. He'd murmur "Benedicite" and hasten along like some fiery prophet or preacher eager to reach his pulpit. We went through the cloisters where the calligraphers and scribes were gathering for a fresh day's work. Quills were being sharpened. Parchments, laid out with weights on the corners, were being vigorously brushed and smoothed with pumice-stones. Ink powders were being mixed. Brilliant paints: gold, red, green and scarlet poured out into pots. They gleamed magnificently in the powerful sunlight. Anselm scarcely gave them a second glance, but hurried on past the church. We hastily crossed gardens where flowers moved like a sea of colour in all their summer glory. We slithered over stable-yards awash with dung and wet straw, where dogs barked and chickens foraged hungrily for seed. At last we reached the Long Meadow, a lonely stretch of grassland which runs from the back of the Abbey down to a tree-lined pond fed by a tributary of the Stour. Usually the Abbey cattle graze there but on that particular day the great meadow was empty except for a tall, burly lay-brother, head shorn and dressed in a dirty-stained robe with a coarse rope around his waist. Beside him stood a wheelbarrow containing bows, quivers of arrows, as well as two ugly arbalests or crossbows. About seven yards away, a make-shift butt or target had been slung on a pole for all to see, a small, round shield on which circles had been painted. Anselm introduced Oderic, formerly a farmer and bowman as well as a veteran of Senlac. He had been one of those archers who'd brought Harold Godwinson's house-carls and fyrd under a ferocious hail of arrows. Oderic had sharp, green eyes, his leathery skin wrinkled and furrowed, his nose slightly broken. He spoke the patois in a harsh, lilting voice and declared that he was just a poor lay-brother, though he grinned when Anselm complimented him on his bow and the accuracy of his aim. Anselm asked for his advice and Oderic rose to the bait. In truth he was a Magister or Peritus, a skilled practitioner of archery. He was also a man who truly loved the sound of his own voice. He lectured us on the different bows and the ugly arbalest with its heavy frame, powerful winch and sharpened bolts. He then moved on to the small bow, the composite bow, the arrows with their feathery flights and wicked, barbed tips. He demonstrated how to judge the wind, calculate the distance, the need for discipline, as well as protection with leather finger-guards and stout, metal-embossed braces around his powerful wrists. I stood and listened, aware of the sounds of the Abbey, the lowing of cattle herded in their pens, the thronging songs of blackbirds and thrushes. Oderic, on Anselm's instruction, concentrated on the bow the Red King and his party must have used that fateful evening. The composite bow was powerful, its stave made up of different sheaves of wood clamped together with horn, glue, cord and sinew. Oderic plucked the powerful twine to hum like the string of a harp, then selected a shaft. He turned, feet slightly apart and loosed shaft after shaft, mere blurs in the summer air as they streaked towards the target striking it dead in the centre at each turn. Anselm leaned on his stick watching fascinated.

"Very good, very good," he murmured. Oderic stood, bow down, chest heaving.

"Tell me Oderic." Anselm pointed to the wood across the

pond, a dark forbidding clump of trees. "If you and I went there to hunt deer, as we soon could, if you wished to ..." He paused, smiling to himself. Father Anselm would never hunt. He hated such cruelty. Once, whilst out riding, a group of horsemen had met us on the highway, a hare they had hunted to exhaustion was sheltering beneath Anselm's horse. Our good Father had laughingly declared it had taken sanctuary, so he insisted that it must go free. Anselm was keen on such kindness. He often declared that abuse towards animals came directly from the Evil One.

"Father?" Oderic gasped wiping his mouth on the back of his hand.

"Drink!" Anselm urged. "Go on Oderic, help yourself to that small wine-skin." He pointed to the barrow. "You've hidden it beneath that leather sheet."

"Father, how did you know?"

Anselm licked a finger as if he were a master bowman and held it up against the breeze. "Not a divine revelation, it's simply that wine, especially Bordeaux, is rich and heavy and its fragrance, like God's grace, quickly spreads out."

Oderic, grinning from ear to ear, unearthed the wine-skin, pulled out its stopper, took a gentle swig and offered it to us. We refused. The lay-brother took another gulp and put it away.

"So Oderic," Anselm continued, "we are in the woods, hunting deer."

"Like the Red King?" Oderic's voice was so harsh he made me jump.

"Sharp, sharp," Anselm agreed, "as the Red King was. Now, Oderic, the verderers and beaters would drive the game between us. You would stand on one side of the glade and me on the other, then ..."

"No, no – " Oderic interrupted lifting his bow, " – that would be stupid, Master. In a hunt you never stand opposite another bowman, the chance of a mishap would be too great. If I missed

– " he shrugged, " – I would certainly hit you."

"True, true!" Anselm intervened. "That's what I thought you'd say. We'd stand on the same side wouldn't we?"

"Of course." Oderic replied. "I've served as a verderer, a forester. I know the ways of the wood and how to organise a day's hunting. The deer are not driven between two lines of men but past a line of men."

"And?"

Oderic lifted his bow in imitation. "Each man chooses his target, usually the quarry's lower neck, and looses. If he misses the chosen target the shaft may still hit the beast's flank or belly."

"Whilst one deer," Anselm commented, "may receive two or even three arrows from the huntsmen it passes. The poor animal slows down and the dogs are released. So, Oderic," Anselm paused, "for sake of argument, Tirel, who allegedly loosed the killing shaft, was standing opposite or away from the King. Is it possible that he missed, the arrow grazed the animal then struck the King directly in the heart?"

Oderic pulled a face, he was clearly uneasy at this questioning, turning the matter over in his mind. Anselm gestured at me.

"What do the Chronicles say, Eadmer?"

"That the King was facing the west, shading his eyes against the setting sun. The arrow struck him in the heart. He broke the shaft off as he fell. Some say the arrow glanced off a tree or the hide of a deer."

"Impossible!" Oderic broke in. He had clearly made his mind up. "It's hard enough to strike a man in the heart, but an arrow, like any missile, loses its force, if it glances off something else."

"Eadmer." Anselm blinked like an owl caught in the open. "Eadmer, you read all the accounts, imitate, play the mummer, what did the Red King do when he was struck?"

I gasped.

"Oh." Anselm leaned hard on his walking stick. "You're not breaking God's commandments or Canon Law – do so!"

I stood back and clutched my chest. I made out as if I was breaking off a shaft embedded deep in my chest, then I acted as if I was falling forward.

"According to one source," I remarked flushed with embarrassment, "the King fell forward driving the shaft deeper into his chest."

"Well?" Anselm turned to Oderic. "And don't," he teased, "say all things are possible!"

"It could happen," Oderic conceded "but if a shaft was embedded so deep it would have to be directly aimed. Falling on such an arrow would drive it further in through the chest." Oderic rubbed the front of his gown. "This is all muscle and bone, warriors can survive an arrow to the chest."

"Then the shaft must have been loosed by someone standing or kneeling facing the King." I mused. "That would make sense. The King was facing the west, the setting sun would blind him, but not the person looking at him."

"Domine." Oderic used Anselm's official title. "Domine, that may not be so. As I have said, you never stand opposite another bowman. Moreover, the King and whoever was with him were hunting deer: these were fleeing for their lives. The dust thrown up would be as thick as any mist."

"Ah yes, I see," Anselm declared. "Yes, I see. If the man responsible was standing opposite, which you think wouldn't happen anyway, the deer thundering by would throw up forest dust and leaves, and cloud his vision, making the target, as well as the King, more difficult to hit."

"There is one other matter," Oderic plucked up the wine-skin. "At Senlac, Harold Godwinson and his men were roaring drunk. You know that don't you? They feasted the night before on stoups of ale, beer and wine."

"Ah, I catch your meaning," I intervened. "Rufus and his

companions had also been drinking, possibly very heavily – they would not be as careful."

"Or as skilful," Anselm intervened. "Brother Oderic." He bowed. "When you return to the Abbey, I will have a small tun of wine, the best from the vineyards outside of Bordeaux, sent to your cell."

"Domine," Oderic spread his hands, "I give you thanks."

"But not all in one gulp!" Anselm quipped. He bade the lay-brother farewell and, plucking me by the sleeve, led me back to our chamber in the Abbey. We walked in silence. Only when I closed the door behind us did Anselm lift his head, his face bright with excitement.

"The bowman, Tirel, or whoever he was, must have stood on the same side as the King, perhaps behind but not opposite him. The deer thunder by – " Anselm walked up and down, " – the King aims, he misses, if one account is to be believed his bow string breaks. He turns and – " Anselm paused, fingers to his lips, " – yes, his bow-string snapped, very strange! Anyway, the Red King turns to Tirel and, as some sources relate, shouts what was it? 'Loose at the devil' or words to that effect. Tirel, wine-soaked, shoots an arrow but the King virtually steps into its path. At such close range the arrow, penetrates deeply, the King falls face down, driving the barb in further."

"So it was an accident?" I asked.

"So it seems, so it seems," Anselm sat down on the stool. "So it seems," he repeated. "As you know Eadmer, I have always striven to be logical. Logic is my great passion and the logic of events all point to the Red King's death being an accident, an unfortunate incident which occurred on 2nd August in the year of Our Lord's incarnation, 1100. Yet, here in my heart, my emotions dictate something else – so what is the truth?" He placed his walking stick on the ground and put his face in his hands. A bell tolled the hours, sombre and low. Anselm rose to his feet.

"Eadmer, lend me your arm. We'll join the good brothers

in the choir and sing God's praises."

We made our way out to the great cloister with its grey pillars, columns, low walls, statutes and gargoyles. The garth greenery was drying in the sun. In the centre sprouted a beautiful rose bush, its flowers full, red and rich. Other monks flittered by like ghosts, eager to reach the cool, incensed church. Anselm paused at the entrance to the garth and stared at the rose bush.

"You know, Eadmer, when I wrote my book *Cur Deus Homo* – 'Why God became Man – I stood in a place like this and realised the full truth. Christ became incarnate not just to save us from our sins. More importantly he wanted to be with us. He found his joy to be with the sons of men. He wanted to experience the fullness of humanity, to discover for himself what it was like to stand in the sun, smell a flower, drink a goblet of wine, go fishing in a boat, enjoy sea breezes, dance at a wedding party. He wanted to experience the sheer joy, the music of life and yes – " Anselm cleared his throat, " – yes, that is what the great Augustine talked about, the music of life, beautiful, thrilling, but sometimes slightly off-key." Anselm glanced at me. "That is what sin does: it disturbs the harmony of life. Sometimes such discordance can even drown the music." He drew closer, resting on my arm. "So it is now with this present business. William Rufus had the making of a great King. In time he may have become one. So who cut short his life? Who sent him unshriven before God's throne? Come!" he urged. "Let us at least sing for his soul."

We entered the church through the Galilee porch, turning right up towards the dramatic Rood screen depicting the Crucifixion of Christ, with Mary and John looking helplessly on. The nave rose above us, lofty arches, masses of stone pushed up like a prayer to almighty God. The transepts and chancery chapels guarded by squat round pillars, were hidden in shadows, but the nave was bathed in the glorious sunlight pouring through the different windows, some plain, others coloured, so it seemed the glory of God was about to break out. Other monks went before us. A few pattered behind, some of them were praying, others less vigilant of the prior and sub-prior, indulged in hushed, quick conversation. Anselm crossed himself as we made our way into the sanctuary and up into the oaken choir stalls. The sedilia were pulled back. A young, fresh-faced brother had the psalters open for us. Anselm and I genuflected towards the sanctuary light glowing in its fiery red glass beneath the silver, jewel-encrusted Pyx. My master refused to sit, but stood and chanted the psalms of the day. One verse distracted me, the cry of David after he had taken Bathsheba and killed her husband Uriah the Hittite.

> Have mercy on me God in your great Kindness, in your infinite compassion, blot out my offence. Oh wash me more and more from guilt and cleanse me from my sin. My offences truly I know them. My sin is always before me. Against you, you alone have I sinned. What is evil in your sight I have done.

The reason for my distraction was that when Anselm reached these verses, he fell silent, closing his eyes and I wondered what he was thinking. God forgive me, but I know my master. He is a man dedicated to the truth, for all his faults and sometimes petty ways. Worry weighed heavy on his heart. Why should one particular verse make him pause, distract him so much? Did Anselm believe that, in the New Forest amongst its oaks and sycamores with the red, fallow deer thundering through the long, lush, green grass, a terrible sin had occurred? And if it did, why should it bother Father Anselm some eight years later?

Once the service was over we joined the rest of the brothers in the refectory, eating bread smeared with honey and jugs of watery ale whilst a lector read from the writings of St Ambrose. Afterwards we took the air then returned to our chamber. For a while Anselm simply walked up and down humming beneath his breath. I was surprised. I recognised the tune, not a hymn but a Goliard song of the Wandering Scholars, a heart-pricking lament about a young man being homesick for some maid he'd left far behind. At last Anselm paused. He went across, opened and closed the heavy chest, then adjusted the crucifix so it hung straight on the lime-washed wall. I was about to ask what was the matter, when there was a sudden knock on the door. Anselm hastened across, opened it and ushered in Brother Jerome, the Librarian. I stifled a groan. Brother Jerome is as talkative as a cricket on a summer's day. I have known saintly brothers feign sleep so he would pass them by. A tall austere man, his chin tucked into his chest with his spiky hair and peculiar stance, Brother Jerome always reminds me of a heron ever ready to dart his pointed nose and lecture anyone unfortunate enough to fall into his toils.

"Father Anselm." Jerome spoke as if delivering a homily in church. "I have consulted the charts and maps. I have taken the Saxon names rather than the Latin ..." He suddenly noticed me, widened his eyes and sniffed disapprovingly as if I'd stolen one of his precious manuscripts.

"Well, Brother." Anselm stretched out his hand expectantly. "You have studied the charts and maps?"

"Yes, Domine, it shows the routes from Gloucester to Brockenhurst, and from there to Winchester and Pevensey. Now that is using the old Roman roads, but should you wish ..."

"Thank you Brother, but I don't want to keep you." Anselm took the piece of parchment from the Librarian's hand. "I mean, if Father Prior is going to inspect the Library."

"Is he?"

"Undoubtedly!"

Brother Jerome fled through the door as if chased by a horde of demons.

"Is Father Prior going to inspect the Library today?" I asked.

"I don't think so."

"Domine," I teased, "you lied."

"Domine, I did not," Anselm retorted. "I simply said the Prior would inspect the Library, as he undoubtedly will sometime, as it is laid down by the Book of Customs drawn up by the Blessed Benedict, founder of our Order. Now – Lord Tirel, Lord of Poix, Chatelain of Pontoise." Anselm sat and peered up at me. "What is the matter, Eadmer, you sit perched on that high stool like a hungry crow on a harvest gate? You have something on your mind?"

"Tirel," I retorted, "is a Frenchman. Didn't you know him at Bec when you were a monk? Has he not dined with you? Why not ask him yourself? Invite him here?"

"Who says I haven't?" Anselm replied. "Yes, I know the Lord of Poix. However, in this matter, until I have finished, all men are strangers to me, especially Tirel. If he accidentally killed the King, why did he flee? Why didn't he stand his ground and let the truth speak for itself?"

"When Richard, the bastard son of Duke Robert, was killed in the May of that same year," I retorted, "the man responsible feared the vengeance of the dead prince's friends and retainers, so he fled for sanctuary to the monastery at Lewes, where he hastily took vows as a monk, assuming the cowl." I gestured at the memorandum I'd drawn up lying on a nearby table. "When the Red King was buried at Winchester, the ribauds and bawds, who lurked in the King's household, would have inflicted their displeasure on their Royal Master's slayer. After all, Tirel was not a subject of the King but a Frenchman. There was no-one to protect him."

"And yet," Anselm intervened, "this Frenchman, this visitor to the English Court, escaped unscathed. No-one stopped him. He was not even detained for questioning?"

"Domine, remember confusion reigned after the King's sudden slaying."

"Still," Anselm murmured, "this Frenchman, during the hours of darkness could flee through a tangled forest across miles of strange countryside to Pevensey. And there was no pursuit? He apparently entered the port and secured safe passage across the Narrow Seas?"

"He had been in England some time, probably since the King's return from France the previous year. He might have grown accustomed – "

"At the dead of night," Anselm interrupted, "a stranger, a foreigner not pursued after slaying a King?"

"One Chronicle does admit that some of the court helped Tirel. They felt sorry for him, they wanted to protect him – after all, it was an accident."

"Wanted to help him?" Anselm smiled, "At a time when other Chronicles claim every man was looking out for himself? A few, God knows who, gave this stranger, this Frenchman, who had just slain their King, albeit accidentally, help and assistance through the forest and down to the coast to take ship to France? No port-reeve, harbour-master, sheriff or bailiff attempted to stop him? No captain of a cog refused him passage?" I didn't answer, the logic of what Father Anselm had said descended like a cloak about me.

"Oh – " Anselm waved a hand, " – I know about the legends already growing up: of a stream Tirel was supposed to have galloped over; about a smithy he stopped at, so his horse could be shoed; but, in the end, he escaped, without hindrance or hurt after killing a King. Why?" Anselm turned and sifted amongst the manuscripts. "William was killed to the south of Brockenhurst, allegedly on a site where a church once stood, another building, a hallowed one, cleared away so that the Conqueror and his family could enjoy their hunting preserve free of interference. Listen." Anselm plucked up a piece of parchment. I didn't recognise it as one I had seen.

"Father Anselm, so you did not give me everything?" Anselm's eyes crinkled in amusement as he glanced at the manuscript.

"Eadmer, I can honestly say, as God is my witness, I did not give you everything, but there is a reason for this. I've told you. I don't wish to overwhelm you." He winked at me. "Let your free will reach its considered decision. Anyway, listen to this extract from one Chronicle. Anselm cleared his throat: "'It is true that upon 2nd August, as the King was hunting in the New Forest, in a place called Througham, all of his company scattered from him except a French knight whose name was Walter Tirel. The King struck a stag with an arrow, which was not greatly hurt and ran away. The King held up his hand shading his eyes against the sun and was unaware that Walter Tirel was also shooting: his arrow glanced against a tree and struck the King in his breast. He hastily broke off what stuck out of his body and, with only a groan, collapsed and died. On this sudden chance his followers, once they understood, fled away. A few of those who remained laid his body into a charcoal burner's cart which was drawn by one lean beast.'" Anselm put the piece of parchment down and picked up one of the charts Brother Jerome had brought. "Yes – that is the place he died – Througham." He mused. "Througham lies to the south-east of Brockenhurst, a good ride on a warm summer's evening." He muttered something under his breath, put the parchment back and turned and stared at the sun pouring through the narrow window. I felt impatient and a little annoyed, yet Father Anselm was like that. He'd ask me to do a task, but then do it himself. Had he withheld other manuscripts?

"So you think the Red King's death is suspicious?" I asked.

"Highly so," Anselm replied, turning round. "Before the conquest, Eadmer, and the custom still persists in England, each shire is roughly divided into hundreds, which in turn, are made up of units of tens or tithings. Each tithing or hundred has a leader who answers for any crime, particularly 'Murdrum', murder or any suspicious death which occurs within his jurisdiction. Well – " he fingered the cord round his waist, " – the Red King on the day of his death had no real kith and kin but me. William was a member of my tithing: I am his frank-pledge." He smiled. "Once, when I was in dispute with the King, I compared us both to two oxen pulling a plough – Church and Kingdom. I must do justice to my fellow ox! St Paul writes that in this life we see the truth only through a veil darkly, but this does not prevent us, Brother, from peering through that veil, searching for the truth. Never forget that famous syllogism: 'Whatever is true is right and whatever is right is just, therefore truth is justice." He walked over and patted me on the arm. "That is, what is at issue here, first the truth but, in God's good time, also justice. Strange," he mused, "as I approach the vespers of my life I return to the matins of my existence: my early days in Val D'Aosta, high in the Alps. I remember all the stories about that place. How the great warrior Hubert the White-Handed won the region for himself through fierce struggle and bloody warfare. A brooding splendid place, Eadmer. My sister Richera and I loved nothing better than to climb its tortuous track-ways and behold what the Ancients used to call the Mountains of Jupiter. Anyway …" Anselm was now lost in what he called the "sweet memories of his childhood". "In those mountains runs a deep and gloomy gorge cut deep into the rock, the drop must be like that between heaven and hell. At the bottom of it thunder rushing waters. This gorge or cleft is crossed by a single causeway. I have always considered the bridge spanning that terrifying gulf as a parable of life. Imagine, Eadmer, as if in a vision, a gorge broad, deep and gloomy. At the bottom of it lie all kinds of instruments of torture. Imagine this valley is spanned by a single bridge, no more than a foot in width. Suppose that this bridge, so narrow, high and dangerous, has to be crossed by one whose eyes are bandaged so he cannot see a step in front of him. His hands are bound behind his back in chains, so it is impossible for him to feel his way with a stick. What horror, what agony of soul, would he experience? Would he find any joy, peace or pleasure? I don't think so. Bereft of pride, emptied of vain glory, his whole soul would be shrouded with the dire blackness of that horrid darkness which comes from the apprehension of death. In addition, suppose that monsters and savage birds hovered above and about the bridge seeking to drag him down into the abyss? Would not his fear be enhanced into soul-chilling terror? Suppose again that his retreat is cut off as he advances. The ground slipping away from under his very feet! Would not the anxiety of our wayfarer be greatly increased? Now learn the meaning of this parable. Brace your mind. The dark, gloomy abyss is hell, immeasurably deep, it is shrouded by a hideous veil of murky darkness and is replete with all kinds of instruments of torture, nothing there alleviates its horror, everything exists to terrify, to excruciate and torture the soul. Everyone who crosses that perilous bridge must do so warily or be hurled into the abyss. The crossing represents our present life. Those who are imprudent, fall and go down into the pit. The portion of the causeway which slips away from under the heel of the wayfarer are the days of our life, they fly away never to return, whilst their rapidly diminishing number urges us ever forward to our goal. The savage birds and malignant beasts which hover around the bridge to lure the travellers to their destruction, are fiends whose evil minds and wills are totally bent on misleading men and casting them into the depths of hell. The wayfarers are, of course, blinded with the thick darkness of ignorance, our wills bound by a heavy chain of sin. We find it difficult to pursue righteousness, to direct our steps freely to God by living a holy life. Consider then, if we are in so critical a position we should, with all our might, cry to God that, fortified by his help, we may advance in confidence through the enemy host. We should remember the holy psalm, 'the Lord is my life, my salvation so whom shall we fear?' Or, as St Paul says, 'Si Deus, Quis Contra, – If God is with us who shall be against?' Now, Eadmer – " Anselm coughed, cleared his throat and gripped his stomach, flinching at the pain, " – remember what I have just said, it is most pertinent to our business here. Yes – " he nodded vigorously, " – very pertinent indeed. You see, Brother, if murder did occur, it was one of those sins which cry out to God for vengeance. If that is true, and I believe it is, how much more the death of a King, the

Lord's anointed, especially one christened, blessed, hallowed in Church, not only by the Head of the Church of England but a man whom I regard as my Magister, my Dominus, the venerable Lanfranc? The Red King, even if all his sins were of the deepest scarlet, was bequeathed to my care by the man I regard as my Lord, my mentor, my friend. Do you remember, Eadmer, when the blessed Lanfranc asked my views on Aefleg, a former Archbishop of Canterbury, a Saxon who was slain by the Danes? Lanfranc wondered if Aefleg could be considered a true martyr because he was murdered after he refused to allow his captors to demand a ransom from his flock, saying the burden would be too great for them. Lanfranc queried whether Aefleg's circumstances made him a true martyr according to the teaching of the Church? I wrote back …" he paused. "What did I write, my memory fails me now?"

I climbed down from the stool and opened the coffer chest containing copies of Anselm's correspondence. They are numbered by year, small scrolls of vellum stitched tightly together. I soon found the correct one, unrolled it and searched out a copy of that letter.

"Well, Eadmer? I begin that letter, don't I, with the words, 'It is manifest …'"

"Yes, Domine," I replied, "you write: 'It is manifest that he who does not hesitate to die rather than commit even a slight sin against God, would, a fortiori, not hesitate to die rather than offend God by a grave sin. It certainly seems to be a graver sin to deny Christ than being an earthly lord who refuses to lay a certain burden on one's people for the ransom of one's life. However, if this latter is a lesser sin, it was one Aefleg refused to commit. Accordingly, if he refused to commit a minor sin, he would certainly not deny Christ, had his opponents demanded that of him. Hence he was a true martyr.'"

I glanced up. "And its bearing on this matter?"

"If murder has been committed – " Anselm declared as if

reciting a syllogism, passion thrilling his voice, " – a great sin has been committed. If the murder is regicide, then that sin is even more grievous. Now I have established that a great mystery surrounds the death of the Red King so, what is my responsibility? If I suspect anything wrong, however petty, and yet do nothing, I am, by force of logic, surely guilty of a grievous sin? To kill is one thing, to kill a king and to conceal that crime is even worse. So to go back to my parable, I am near the end of that perilous bridge; the causeway behind me is slipping away. I regard this mystery as the one last great danger threatening my crossing. Abel's blood cried out for vengeance, so does that of Rufus. I must use all my power, logic and reason, and with the help of God, establish the truth of the matter. I can not give up, give way, just to accommodate my own ease. I am in the vespers of life, Eadmer – my end is near. I have fought the good fight. I have run the race. I have kept faith and I will do so until my dying day. So let's begin, but first ..." Anselm went across to the battered prie-dieu before the crucifix, knelt down and intoned one of his favourite prayers: 'Lux quae luces in tenebris' – 'Light which glows in the deepest shadows.'

I studied that bowed figure and quietly acknowledged that this was not some mere logical exercise. Anselm truly accepted for many reasons the question posed to all of us by God – 'Am I my brother's keeper?' Anselm's answer, as far as William the Red King was concerned, was a resounding 'yes'. My master rose, came across and sat down on the stool.

"Domine?"

"Yes, Eadmer?"

"You are Archbishop, you exercise authority, you have the right to question people."

"I can and I will, Brother, but as regards the evidence ..." He shook his head. "In the main, after so many years, that is now carved in stone; those who supplied it will not revoke their witness, churchmen included. Nobody can change their account, they must accept the established story. If they do change or even try to do so, they might incriminate themselves. No, Brother, this is now a matter of strict logic." He rubbed his hands together. "If it was not an accident, could it be a murder? Walter Tirel is depicted as the slayer – so, if he committed murder, was he acting for himself or others?"

"If he were acting on his own – *sua sponte*," I replied. "What profit was in it for him? What motive? According to the evidence of the day, Walter Tirel was very friendly with the Red King, on the most cordial terms, so why should he kill his royal master, then flee? There is no evidence of any reward or advancement being offered to him later. Also, if it was a murderous slaying, wouldn't the others have stopped him, arrested him? Moreover Tirel does, I understand, through his wife, Adelicia de Clare, hold estates at Langham in Essex. If he'd been hired by someone else, if he had no motive in killing for himself but did it for others, why hasn't he returned to England to claim that reward let alone revisit his estates in Essex?"

"True, true," Anselm replied, picking at his teeth, "and this can be applied to any others in that hunting party, be it King Henry or Tirel's brothers-in-law, the de Clares. Nothing, either before the Red King's death or after it, ties Tirel to them or any profit whatsoever. Perhaps Tirel was acting for someone like Philip of France whose territory the Red King threatened, or his brother, Duke Robert, returning from the Crusade with a new wife and, more importantly, a rich dowry, which he'd use to pay his debts and buy back his mortgaged duchy?" Anselm shook his head. "Again, there's no evidence whatsoever that Tirel was acting for them or anyone else. So, *cui bono*, who profits from the Red King's death, who, Eadmer?"

"Perhaps there is evidence – we just haven't found it – particularly about the like of Philip of France and Helias la Flèche, Count of Maine? They must have been alarmed about the Red King's victories abroad, his possible acquisition of the Duchy of

Aquitaine – after all, William did boast he'd celebrate Christmas in Poitiers – perhaps he saw himself as a new Charlemagne, sweeping all before him?"

"Festina Lente – let's hasten and slowly," Anselm retorted. "The Red King may have entertained grandiose plans, but a full campaign against Philip of France would have been costly both in men and treasure. William would have to leave England and Normandy. True, last year he went to war against Count Helias, but he didn't have it all his own way, did he? Helias remained stubborn, Philip of France equally so, in defending their seigneuries – why should they stoop to murder? More importantly, why should Sir Walter Tirel be another person's assassin? If he tried and failed, it would mean an excruciating death. If he succeeded, the same fate. He could never have guessed he would escape so easily. Moreover, Tirel was castellan of a strategically placed fortress in the Vexin, he opened this to William. He'd become the Red King's friend, his boon companion in peace and war, so how could Philip of France, or anyone else, suborn such a man? What profit was there in it for Tirel? So, let's turn to others – who else profited from the Red King's death?"

"Well it's obvious," I replied, "Henry, his younger brother. He became King almost immediately."

Anselm rounded his eyes. "But that was a mere gamble," he declared. "Surely Henry had no guarantee before his brother died that he would be King. There is no document, no public declaration saying that he was the heir apparent? Remind me, Eadmer, what happened on that night of 2nd August, and on the subsequent days when Henry proclaimed himself as King and hurried to London to be crowned?"

I climbed down from the high stool. I went across and picked up the memorandum I'd drawn up, and returned, unrolling it and using weights to keep it in position, until I found the passage: "On 2nd August, 1100 ..." I used my finger moving it from word to word.

"No, no!" Anselm interrupted. "Tell me first what happened beforehand, I mean between the Red King and Prince Henry."

I glanced up. "Master, that is easy enough: eight years before Rufus died, Henry rebelled against him. However, by the end of 1092, Henry and his brother, the Red King had reached a rapprochement, they became allies against their elder brother, Robert, but that was always the case. Do you remember, Father Anselm, an incident from their youth?"

"Ah, yes." Anselm nodded slowly.

"It happened during the campaign season of 1078, almost 30 years ago." He reminisced. "William the Conqueror and his three sons were staying in a town. The King had one house, Robert and his retinue the other. William was about 18, Henry, about ten. The younger brothers, William and Henry, visited Robert and went upstairs to play soldiers. Apparently they made a great commotion and started throwing water out of the window down on their elder brother Robert and his friends. Robert became furious, for he'd been drinking, and dashed up the stairs. The broil which ensued was so fierce it brought the King on the scene. He restored order and forced them to make friends but Robert thought he'd been insulted; he withdrew and actually went to war against his own father. The Conqueror never forgot that. Years later, when the Red King had been on the throne for about five years, Henry tried to rebel against both his brothers, William of England and Robert of Normandy, but he was forced to submit. He later allied himself to the Red King and, by 1094, he was actually being paid by William to wage war against Robert in Normandy. In 1086 when Normandy passed into the Red King's possession, Henry received certain counties including Bayeux."

"And on the day the Red King was killed, and afterwards?"

"Henry was apparently hunting in the New Forest when men hastened to him, one after another, informing him of his brother's death. You've read my account. According to popular belief, Henry had been sheltering in a hut mending his bow-string.

One story I remember, was how an old woman approached him and prophesied that he was not just the Red King's brother, a Count, but soon to be King himself. According to one source when Henry learnt about his brother's death, he grieved and actually went to where the body lay. Others claim he hastened immediately to Winchester where the royal treasures are stored, and demanded the keys of the kingdom from the guard. A leading nobleman, William de Breteuil, refused to hand them over, declaring that Duke Robert was Henry's elder brother and therefore the rightful heir. The dispute became fierce. Men came running to the spot, many took the Count's part. Henry placed his hand on his sword, drew it, and declared that no-one should stand between him and his father's sceptre. Friends and nobles gathered round and, after fierce discussion, the treasury was eventually delivered to Prince Henry. The next day the royal council were present and, after much discussion, they chose Henry as King, mainly due to the influence of the Beaumont Brothers, Henry, Earl of Warwick and his elder brother Robert of Beaumont, Count of Meulan. This was Friday 3rd August. By Sunday 5th August, Henry was at Westminster, where he was crowned by Maurice, Bishop of London as you, Master, were still in exile."

Anselm smiled and nodded. "Your account," he murmured, "seems to prove my point, that Henry's succession to the throne was not smooth or expected. Indeed, according to you, Henry had to struggle for the first six years of his reign to establish himself." He wagged a finger at me. "I shall, my dear Eadmer, ask you to go back to that, whilst hunting, but for the moment, do continue with your account."

"At his coronation, Henry swore to give peace to both Church and people, to act justly and establish good laws. On the same day, he published a charter which declared that he had been made King by common consent of the Lords, and revoked all evil customs introduced during the last reign. The Church was to be free, its offices and revenues were neither to be sold nor farmed out. At the same time, Father Anselm, shortly after his coronation, Henry wrote to you, inviting you to return, declaring that he committed himself to you, the counsel of the Bishops and those others whose right it was to advise him. Henry promised to reform all abuses and after listening to the advice of the Bishops, married Princess Mathilda, crowning her Queen at Westminster Abbey on 11th November 1100."

"A beautiful woman," Anselm murmured, "hair like gold, skin as soft as the whitest snow. They say that she and Henry had loved each other for years." He sighed. "I thought it would bring an end to his lustful concupiscence." Anselm's voice trailed off. He sat staring across the chamber. I could almost guess his thoughts. Henry the King was hot and lecherous as a sparrow in spring. He had a cohort of mistresses and enough bastard children to fill a small hall. Henry had married in November 1100, Mathilda, baptised Edith, daughter of the Scottish King. She had already borne him children, a daughter also called Mathilda and a lusty boy William. Marriage to a beautiful woman and the birth of healthy children had not cooled the new King's lechery. In truth, Anselm always had doubts about the validity of Henry and Mathilda's marriage, these regularly surfaced as they did then.

"Read to me, Eadmer – " Anselm turned back to the candle, " – what you wrote at the time of the Queen's marriage."

"Mathilda – " I began when I found the place in my history, " – the daughter of Malcolm, the noblest King of Scots and known to be descended from the ancient Kings of the Saxons, married Henry, King of England. Her mother, Margaret, was the daughter of Edward, son of King Ethelred, who in turn was descended from the glorious King Edgar. Although the question of this marriage has, as some may think, no bearing on the intended purpose of my work." I glanced up. Anselm smiled.

"Always the gossip, Eadmer!"

I shrugged and returned to the manuscript. "The matter was handled by Father Anselm, who confirmed their marriage with his blessing and also consecrated her as Queen. I must briefly describe how this came about. I am particularly anxious to do so because quite a large number of people have maligned Anselm." I paused as my master once again whispered St Paul's famous verse: 'Si Deus quis contra?' – 'If God is with us who shall be against?'

"A large number of people," I repeated, "had maligned Anselm saying, as we ourselves have heard them, that in this matter he did not keep to the path of strict justice. Certainly this is not true. Mathilda was raised up from early childhood in a convent of nuns and grew there into womanhood. Many believed her father had dedicated her to God's service as she'd often been glimpsed wearing the veil, like the nuns with whom she lived. After she had discarded her veil but not her vows, as she had not taken any, Prince Henry fell in love with her. This sent many tongues wagging, it hindered the truth, and prevented both from embracing one other as they desired. Accordingly, all looked to Anselm for a solution in this matter. Was Mathilda free to marry the new King? Princess Mathilda went and humbly beseeched Anselm's advice and assistance on the issue. My master, referring to the rumours swirling about, declared that he would not be persuaded, by any argument, to take God's bride away from him and join her in marriage to an earthly Prince. Mathilda passionately denied she'd ever been consecrated as a nun. She also denied that she'd had ever, at any time, taken the convent veil by her own consent. She declared that if it was necessary to persuade Anselm she would prove this before the judgement seat of the entire English Church. 'True, I did assume the veil,' Mathilda said, 'I do not deny that, but there was a good reason. When I was a young girl, I went in fear of my Aunt Christina, the Abbess, whom you must know quite well. She, to protect me from the lust of the rapacious Normans who, at that time, were ready to rape any woman, used to put a little black hood over my head. When I threw it off, she would often make me smart with a sharp slapping and a most vitriolic scolding – she would treat me as if I'd done something wrong. So, it is true, I did indeed wear that hood in her presence, yet I resented it most fiercely. As soon as I escaped from her presence, I tore the hood off, threw it to the ground and trampled on it. So in that way, although foolishly, I used to vent my anger, my hatred of it, which constantly welled up inside me. Only in that fashion was I veiled, as my conscience bears witness. True, people claim I was dedicated to God, but as many persons still alive will attest, when my father once visited Wilton and by chance saw me veiled, he snatched the veil off, tore it into pieces and invoked the anger of God upon the person who had put it on me. He declared that he would rather have me marry Count Alan of Richmond than commit me to a house of nuns. So, Reverend Father, that is my reply to the slanders spread abroad about me. I humbly ask your wisdom to reflect on this and to do for me as you, my spiritual father and judge, deem what is right.'"

I glanced up. "Master, shall I continue?"

"Do so," Anselm replied, head down.

"To be succinct, Father Anselm refrained from delivering an immediate decision: he declared that the entire case ought to be decided by the leading churchmen of the realm. So, at Anselm's request, on the appointed day, the bishops, abbots and all the nobles and leading men of the religious professions gathered in the manor of St Andrew of Rochester near Lambeth. Anselm himself attended and put the question before them. The case was discussed in detail. From various sources, credible witnesses came forward to support the young woman's story – in particular, two archdeacons whom Father Anselm had sent to Wilton to make enquiries, and to establish what was known as the truth of the matter. These two archdeacons declared in the hearing of the whole assembly, that they had carried out the most careful enquiries amongst the sisters and they had learnt nothing which was inconsistent with the account the Lady Mathilda had given. Once he heard this, Anselm advised them all, and charging them by their Christian duty of obedience, that none of the assembly should, out of fear or favour, pervert his judgement, but that each churchman, realising this was a matter for God, should discuss to the best of his ability, so that the question could be rightly decided. 'Lest,' Anselm remarked, 'and God forbid that it should be so, you issue a judicial sentence which would set a precedent for the future by either depriving someone of their liberty or defrauding God of what is rightfully His.' All of them, by acclamation, signified that this is what would be done, promising they would not fail in their task.

Anselm then withdrew, and the Assembly of the entire Church of England discussed what their decision should be. When this had been done, Anselm was reverently escorted back to the Assembly to find out the final decision on the matter which they'd all agreed upon and now published. They declared, having carefully investigated, that Princess Mathilda could not in all justice be bound by a decision to prevent her from being free to dispose of her person in whatever way she legally wanted to do.

'Although,' the Fathers said, 'we would have no difficulty in establishing through simple reasoning, yet this is unnecessary because of a decision pronounced in a similar case by your predecessor of blessed memory, our Father and Master Lanfranc. When the Great Duke William first conquered this land, many of his men believed that everything ought to yield and submit to their wicked lusts. They carried out violence, not only against the possessions of the conquered but, where opportunity offered, married and unmarried women alike with disgraceful lechery. Consequently, a number of women, anticipating this and fearing for their own virtue, fled to convents and took the veil to protect themselves from any hurt. After a period of time, when this violence had quietened down and peace had been established, Father Lanfranc was asked what view he took on the treatment of those who had safeguarded their chastity by taking refuge in convents, whether or not they were legally bound to remain in the convent and keep the veil which they had assumed. Lanfranc, with the advice of a General Council, decided the issue by giving judgement that those who had, by their conduct so clearly safeguarded their chastity, should not be forced to remain in the convent unless they chose to do so of their own free will. Some of us, the Assembly declared, actually took part in these proceedings. We witnessed this judgement approved by men of wisdom. Accordingly, we are anxious that this same decision hold good in this present case and ask for it to be confirmed. Mathilda was under compulsion. Nevertheless, so that no-one may think that we are influenced by favour towards anyone, we do not want, in giving judgement to go further, but are content to rest our decision on this precedent alone, that what held good in more serious cases should also hold good in the less serious.'

Anselm, after a period of reflection, replied.

You know the warning and charge I gave you and the assurances you made. Now you have unanimously delivered judgement as seemed to you to be the most just, as you assure me you have I will not reject your judgement. I accept it with all the more confidence as I am told it is supported by the authority of so great a Father as Lanfranc.

Mathilda was then brought before the assembly. She calmly heard and appreciated what had taken place and asked to make a brief, public statement. Mathilda offered to prove by oath, or by any other process of Canon Law, that her story, as already described, was in strict accordance with the truth of the matter. She declared that she would do so, not that they didn't believe her, but to cut away any opportunity for malevolent people to whisper any scandal in the future. The Fathers of the Assembly replied that there was no need for such a declaration: a wicked man spoke out of the evil treasure in his heart and he would be immediately silenced as the truth of the matter had been clearly established by the decision of so many leading prelates."

I put the manuscript down. Anselm sat on his stool rocking

himself gently backwards and forwards. He abruptly stood up as if he'd recalled something important.

"When did we return from exile, Eadmer?" he asked.

"The Red King was killed on 2nd August," I replied. "Messengers were immediately dispatched to us. We landed at Dover on 23rd September and the marriage," I concluded, "took place on 11th November."

"Seven weeks after we returned!" Anselm replied. "I remember it well. Your reading of it, Eadmer, refreshes my memory. The urgency of that young woman to marry the King! I suppose it is understandable – the prospect of being Queen would dazzle any maid's eyes. Yet, notice how your account picks up the flavour of the time: how the Assembly were very quick to point out that the decision they'd reached was without fear or favour. They were, of course, referring to the King."

"What are you implying, Domine?"

"I'm implying, good Brother, that here is a King, newly elected and freshly crowned. He didn't even wait for me to return to consecrate him, but persuaded, or forced Maurice, Bishop of London to do it for me. In the autumn of 1100 Henry faced many problems, but his marriage to that young Mathilda and my return, virtually take precedence over everything. It just makes me wonder."

"What, Master?"

"The true nature of Henry and Mathilda's relationship during the reign of the Red King? They must have kept it very well hidden. Do you know, Eadmer, it is not in your account, but on my return from exile I met Henry privately. He informed me that he'd taken an oath to David of Scotland, Mathilda's brother, that he would marry his sister, which demonstrates how Henry must have acted speedily. William was killed on 2nd August, Henry must have dispatched the fastest courier to Scotland. I can understand the politics. He needed to keep his northern shires safe and protected. The marriage alliance with the Scots would assist that. In the end, however, Henry's marriage to Mathilda was foremost on his mind – why? Did he fear someone else might marry her and beget an heir? After all, Duke Robert was on his way home ..."

"And?"

"Robert visited the Scottish court many years ago. There is a rumour that he was the Queen's godfather. He stood at the font when young Mathilda was baptized – did Henry fear Duke Robert might hinder that marriage? Moreover, until then, there had been no legitimate grandson of the Conqueror. Robert, by his marriage to Sybil, might fill such a gap and enhance even further his own celebrated status. He would be Duke Robert of Normandy, the great Crusader, the father of a legitimate heir, a living obstacle to all Henry's aspirations, including marriage to Mathilda. The late summer of that fateful year was certainly a time for decisive action, so much haste," Anselm murmured, "so much haste."

I put the manuscript down and returned to my stool. "Master, others say differently, that Mathilda did not want to marry the new King?"

Anselm chuckled to himself. He stretched his neck, clasping and unclasping his hands as he always did when embarrassed. Mathilda's marriage to Henry was one of these embarrassments. I suspect my good Father was never really convinced that Mathilda was free to marry. True, he had publicly supported her betrothal, yet from the very beginning he seemed to entertain secret reservations, withdrawing himself from the debate and allowing that Council at Lambeth to reach the decision for him. Once the issue was settled, relations did not improve between Anselm and the Queen. In fact, they remained cool and polite, certainly on my master's part. He never waxed lyrical with her as he did in his correspondence with Gunhilda, daughter of Harold Godwinson, who'd been in the same convent at Wilton as Mathilda. The root of the problem was that 14 years earlier, in the spring of 1094, Anselm had written passionately to the Bishop of Salisbury about both Mathilda and Gunhilda, then young girls, who had been withdrawn from the convent of Wilton so as to marry great noblemen. Anselm insisted that both girls should be returned forthwith as Brides of Christ. This event heavily influenced Anselm's views on Mathilda, even though she publicly denied she had ever assumed the veil. Of course, Queen Mathilda was intelligent enough to realise this, and desperately courted Father Anselm's favour, even describing herself as: 'Filia Anselm Archiepiscopi' – 'Daughter of Anselm, Archbishop'. In 1103 my master quarrelled so furiously with her husband the King that he went into exile again. Queen Mathilda wrote him the most fulsome letters. I quote an extract from one of these:

> You are my joy, my hope, my refuge, [she wrote].
> My soul seeks after you as a man does water in dry land. Accordingly, I stretch out my hand to thee, that you may sprinkle my dryness with the oil of gladness. But, if neither my prayers nor public necessity recall thee, I will eventually put aside my role of dignity, abandon the royal insignia, lay down the symbols of power, despise my crown, tread underfoot my purple and fine linen and come to thee consumed with sorrow.
> I shall embrace thy footsteps and kiss thy feet and no-one shall thrust me away until my desire is fulfilled.

On reflection this fulsome letter received a very chilling reply. Anselm rebuked Mathilda for her treatment of certain churches and the patronage she wielded. He stiffly repelled her nominee to the Abbacy of Malmesbury, despite her regard for the Archbishop's rights, because the unfortunate man had sent him a present. When Anselm fell ill in Normandy in 1106, Mathilda dispatched passionate letters to hear news about his recovery to full health: "For, [she wrote] I shall, and without delay, rejoice in your health which is mine also." My master remained unmoved. Indeed I have seen his last letter to the Queen in which he refused her request to intercede with the King about a plaintiff who had been deprived of his goods: "Because – " as Anselm wrote, " – you know it is not my job to testify about things which I have neither seen nor heard." I have often reflected on that remark. Was it a veiled allusion to Mathilda's true condition before her marriage? Was Anselm saying that he had not, to his own personal satisfaction, seen or heard anything which convinced him that Mathilda was free to marry? The death of the Red King had apparently rekindled such scruples. Anselm rose and walked over to stare down at the hour candle as if treasuring every pearly drop burnt away by the flickering flame.

"Whatever I think," he remarked, "the Norman lords laughed at Henry." He spoke sharply over his shoulder. "They jeered at him for marrying a Saxon princess, instead of taking a Norman bride. They made up nicknames for the royal couple: Leofric or Goderic for Henry, ridiculing him as a Saxon peasant whilst Mathilda was given the name Godgivu." He turned round. "Henry must have truly loved her, at least then."

"They said that," I agreed.

"Though there is no mention of any relationship between them before the Red King died, which means," Anselm continued slowly, "they must have kept the matter well hidden. Why?" He put a finger to his lips. "Because," he answered his own question, "the Red King would certainly not like the idea of his younger brother allying himself to the royal Saxon house."

"Did Rufus contemplate marriage? Did he consider Mathilda for himself?"

"Eadmer, you searched the manuscripts, have you found anything?"

"No," I replied.

"I did!" Anselm smiled and came back resting his hand on the writing desk and peered up at me. "Apparently, seven years before he died, when Mathilda was a girl of some 12 or 13 summers, the Red King came to visit her. Now the Abbess at the time was very upset; she was frightened of the King, he was young and wild and always wanted to do immediately whatever came into his head. He might, when he saw how beautiful Mathilda was, indecently assault her, especially as he arrived so unexpectedly and without notice. Anyway – " Anselm licked his dry lips, " – the Abbess hid Mathilda in a more private chamber. She told the Red King that the girl was consecrated to God and put a veil on her head, so when the King did see her, he'd be deterred from any lecherous embrace. Eventually William came into the cloisters as if he wanted to look at a rosebush flowering there. In truth, he wanted to glimpse Mathilda but as soon as he saw her and the other girls wearing the veil, the King went out of the cloister and left the convent.

Anselm paused, eyes screwed up in concentration.

"So what do we have, Eadmer? Seven years before his death William visited the girl, wondering perhaps if she could be a possible bride?" He laughed sourly, "It's the only time I believe the Red King ever showed any interest in a noble woman as a potential bride, but what William saw, Henry must have also seen. If William could fall in love with her, why not Henry?"

"Domine, who said William fell in love with Mathilda or saw her as a future bride?"

Anselm looked steadily at me.

"Oh no," I gasped, "now I see!"

"What do you see, Brother?"

"I could never understand your opposition to Mathilda marrying Henry, but of course, if she wasn't free to marry a nobleman like Alan de Richmond, she wasn't free to marry the Red King ..."

"Then why, Eadmer, was she suddenly free to marry Henry?" Anselm rubbed his hands together. "Did the Red King, ever force a woman? No! Would he, for all his faults, enter a well-known convent and carry out an assault, the rape of a royal princess, a young maiden of no more than 12 or 13 summers? An act which would have shocked everyone and incurred the most serious sanctions of both Church and State? Of course not! I believe Eadmer, William Rufus went to Wilton to view a possible royal bride but was solemnly assured that she was married to God. Hence my deep suspicions in the autumn of 1100 about Mathilda's betrothal to Henry."

"So Henry was trapped." I replied. "If William couldn't marry Mathilda because she was supposedly a nun, why would he allow his younger brother to do so? In fact," I continued, "and I have searched most carefully, the Red King made little concession to Henry, be it the prospect of the Crown, or a powerful, position and certainly not the hand of Mathilda."

"Yet – " Anselm returned to the point, " – Henry must have loved Mathilda, they must have met?" He shrugged. "He must have wanted to marry her even before that fateful August. First, the way he acted so swiftly once the Red King was dead. Secondly, on the question of his marriage to Mathilda, Henry was willing to risk the resentment and opposition of his Norman lords whose support he so desperately needed at the time. Finally, there's the dog in the manger." Anselm smiled wickedly at me. "You've heard? William de Warrene, Earl of Surrey. Didn't he desire the hand of Mathilda? Wasn't he responsible for mocking Henry before the Red King's death with barbed comments about his appearance and his love of hunting? He could have also been responsible for the hostile whispering campaign against Henry's marriage to Mathilda, born of resentment at what he'd lost, what he had always lusted after. Moreover, as your account proves, Warrene later joined the Norman lords when they rebelled against Henry. He was later pardoned, rather quickly, secretly, probably at Mathilda's behest."

At the time, I wasn't too sure where my master was leading. I climbed down from the high stool and walked across to the window. I peered through at the glorious tapestry of summer, the greenery, the sunlight sparkling in the water in the small fountain bowl, the sky bending overall, a beautiful shade of lady-blue. The sounds of the Abbey echoed faintly, the cut of an axe, the creak of a wheel, muted voices, cattle lowing, dogs snapping and barking, the cooing of dove from their cotes.

"Eadmer?"

"Domine." I glanced back at Anselm. "Quo vadis? Where are you going with all this?"

I put my hands on the sill and relished the coolness of the stone.

"Henry – " I turned round, " – won both Crown and Lady, but that was not a foregone conclusion."

Anselm paced up and down as I emphasised the points on my fingers.

"Primo: No document, no pact or treaty, not even a verbal declaration made Henry the Red King's heir. His elder brother Robert enjoyed a much better claim. My account of events after 1100 clearly prove this. Henry had to face fierce opposition to his accession.

Secundo: Henry had no real patron or supporters either here or abroad, he was a simple lord. You, Master, were crucial to him in achieving the support he did yet, as I have written, right from the start Henry had to face iron-hard opposition. On the night the Red King was killed, he reached Winchester to seize the royal treasure horde. William de Breteuil, the Treasurer, not only opposed him but emphasized the superior claims of his brother, Duke Robert. Swords were drawn; violence was only averted by the very crisis which had occurred. Nonetheless, in the months and years following, Henry had to bribe, intrigue, struggle and face revolt both here and in Normandy. Conspiracy, treason, invasion and betrayal became the norm. True, in the end Henry was victorious. He crushed his enemies at Tinchebrai, captured his brother and confined him to the White Tower outside London. Yet – " I held my hand up, " – six years of battle in all.

Tertio: The leading nobles, men you have invited here:

Fitzhaimo, Henry de Beaumont, Earl of Warwick and his brother Robert, Count of Meulan, as my account describes, later supported Henry, but they were also fervent adherents of the Red King. They would not have stood aside and allowed their royal master to be murdered and then permit the man responsible to succeed to the throne. Robert of Meulan in particular," I continued fiercely, "was one of the few men who had the heart and ear of King William. You know that, Domine! In your struggle against Rufus, Robert of Meulan played a prominent part, countering your arguments, organising your own bishops against you, why should a man like that turn against his King? There is no evidence?"

"True, true," Anselm murmured. "Even when the King went to war against Helias La Flèche and the latter wished to sue for peace and become the King's friend, Meulan prevented it." Anselm snapped his fingers and pointed to the document chest. "There is an account of that isn't there?"

I got down from my stool, opened the ribbed, metal-studded chest, sifted amongst the manuscripts and found the account of events someone had dispatched to Anselm during our exile. Whilst I searched, Anselm crossed to the small table near the lavarium: he poured two generous cups of white wine and brought one over for me.

"Drink," he smiled, "take a little wine for the stomach's sake."

I sipped from the goblet, put it on the ledge and studied the account of how Helias La Flèche had fought the Red King and been captured at Bayeux. On being released from his prison, dark and unshaven, Helias was taken before the King at Rouen and said to him humbly: "'Great King,' I read aloud, 'Ruler over me, help me, I beg you out of your abundant generosity. For long I have enjoyed the title of Count of Maine because I held that fair county by hereditary right. Now, by change of fortune, I have lost both title and county. Therefore, I beg you to receive me into your retinue with the title of my former rank and I will repay you with worthy service. I do not ask for the city of Le Mans or the castles of Maine until I have performed some appropriate service and deserve to receive them back from your royal hand. Until that day, my wish is to be counted among the members of your household and to enjoy your kindly favour.' William the King was prepared to cede this but Robert, Count of Meulan, dissuaded him out of jealous rancour. Robert of Meulan, chief amongst the King's Councillors and Justices, was frightened to allow an equal or superior into the Royal Council Chamber. He argued that the men from the County of Maine were treacherous and achieved through deceit and duplicity, what they could not achieve through force of arms. 'Here is a conquered enemy,' Meulan declared, "making false confession in the hope of being your confidant. Why does he ask for this? I'll tell you, it is in order to draw closer to your secret councils so, when the opportunity favours him, he may rebel all the more savagely and form a deadly alliance with your enemies against you.' On hearing this …" I paused.

"No, no," Anselm whispered, "continue."

"On hearing this," I read, "the King changed his mind. The brave Helias was refused a place in the King's household with the result that many later endured great trials, hardships, dangers and loss. Helias tried to soothe King with fair words, but in vain. 'Very well,' Helias declared, 'I would gladly have served you as my Lord and King. It would have been have my duty and pleasure not to have failed you. So, I ask you not to blame me if I try another course. I cannot patiently stand aside while my inheritance is taken from me. I am denied all justice here. Force alone prevails. Consequently, let nobody be surprised if I champion my claim and strive to recover what is mine by every means in my power.' On hearing this, the King replied: 'But I've got you, sir!' To which Helias replied, 'Only by sheer luck. If I can escape, I know what I am going to do.' 'You do?' The King shouted. He grabbed hold of Helias and shook him with rage. 'Do you think I care what you do, go away, get out, sod off! You can do your damn'dest, and by the face of Lucca, if next time you're the winner, I shall not be asking for something in return …'"

I put the manuscript down and looked up. "Clear proof," I declared, "that Robert of Meulan ruled William's heart. Why should he and his like give that up for Henry, a nonentity with no claim to the throne, who would to have to face opposition, particularly from his brother, Duke Robert, returning home blessed by Holy Mother Church as the Great Crusader?"

Anselm didn't reply, but walked up and down the cell, sipping his wine, talking softly to himself. I recognised his mood. When he was studying his great works, constructing his arguments, looking for proof, testing a hypothesis, he would stride up and down, sometimes in the outer garden or small cloister, talking to himself as if there was some unseen presence which escorted him everywhere. This time however, I was impatient.

"Domine?" I asked.

He paused. I returned to my desk and sat, pen raised, the lid of the ink pot thrown back.

"Your conclusions?" I teased. Anselm drained the wine cup and moved it from hand to hand.

"You are right, Eadmer," he sighed, "Henry gained much, but at the time, that was unknown. He had to face violent opposition and why should the likes of Meulan and Fitzhaimo, be party to the destruction of a King who had served them so very well? Accordingly – " he pursed his lips, " – force of logic leaves one person, one group who did profit beyond all expectations."

"Domine?" Anselm stopped his pacing, his eyes were enlarged, much darker, his face even more pallid. He lifted the earthenware goblet in mock toast. "Why, Brother, myself, the Benedictine Order and, by implication, Holy Mother Church!"

"But you also quarrelled with King Henry!" I retorted. "You fought with him over the rights of the Church."

"But that's all settled now," Anselm declared, "In the year

of Our Lord 1100 it definitely wasn't. I, Archbishop of Canterbury was in exile. Abbacies and bishoprics were empty, their revenues held by the King and," he smiled thinly, "the likes of Magister Flambard who'd got himself appointed to the Bishopric of Durham. He'd also managed to secure the revenues of the vacant Bishoprics of Winchester and Salisbury not to mention at least a dozen abbacies. Pope Urban II had died without the matter between myself and the Red King being resolved, whilst William was openly contemptuous of our new Pontiff Paschal II."

"Domine," I interjected, "what are you implying?"

"Paschal, our Pope, was a Benedictine monk of Vallambrosa, as I am of Bec – William was dismissive of us both." Anselm waved at some manuscripts on the small writing table at the far side of the room. "Remember when we were sheltering in Lyons? Rufus sent an envoy offering new terms to us. I had no choice but to reject them. After that, although the Red King's envoy said another messenger would come, I truly believed I would die in exile, certainly on one particular day. Do you remember, Eadmer, I'd sent you to certain friends in Lyons?"

"I recall it," I agreed "and when I returned, you were sitting by yourself in a lonely cell. You looked completely broken. You dictated a letter which filled me with dread."

Anselm picked up one of the manuscripts from the writing table. "This is a copy of that letter. Copy it again Eadmer, reflect on it, as I have. There is other business I must attend to."

The bells of the Abbey broke in, tolling the hours of the day. I thought my master was going to join the good brothers in church but he grasped the back of my hand, his touch was cold as ice. I stared into his troubled eyes.

"This other business," he whispered, "just copy that down, word for word and reflect upon it, make it part of the memorandum, and when you're finished – " he pointed at his table and another document lying there, " – copy that also, then compare them." He bade me farewell and left.

IV

Terce
Historical Notes

On the location of Rufus' death I have ignored the conventional account on the location of the Rufus stone and accept what Arthur Lloyd, *The Death of Rufus* (New Forest Museum, 2000) argues as the correct location. Anselm's description of life being compared to crossing a dangerous gorge stems directly from his meditations. For the quarrel between the Conqueror's sons – Oderic Vitalis, *Historical Works (Historia Ecclesial Dunelmensis)*, I, (Rolls Series, 1882), Book II, p.356 et. seq. Regarding Henry I's coronation oath – Vaughan, *Anselm of Bec and Robert Meulan* (1987). For the confrontation between the Red King and Helias La Flèche, Oderic Vitalis (op. cit.), V, pp.246-48 and William of Malmesbury, *De Gestis Rerum Anglicorum*, ed. W. Stubbs, (Rolls Series,1887-1889), Vol. II, pp.373-74. As regards Mathilda: Agnes Strickland, *Lives of the Queens of England* (1845), I, p.148 et. seq. The original sources are Eadmer, *Historia Novorum in Anglia* (The Cresset Press, 1964), pp.126 and 131 and *Sancti Anselm Opera Omnia*, ed. F.S. Schmitt (1946-1952), Epp (letters), 317, 320, 400 and 406. Anselm was always very cool towards Mathilda – as if he did not trust her. In the modern idiom, he regarded her as 'too sweet to be wholesome'. I believe Mathilda and Henry were in love before 1100 and, until then, Mathilda used her status as 'veiled' against would-be unacceptable suitors – including Rufus. However, for the right man, at the right time, in the right place, this pretext was dropped, hence Anselm's grave reservations about the entire matter.

V

Sext

It was there he broke the flashing arrows.
(Psalm 75)

I studied the first letter my master indicated. Jesu Miserere – it reads as follows:

"To his Lord and Reverend Father Paschal, Supreme Pontiff, Anselm, slave of the Church of Canterbury, offers due submission. I rejoice and give thanks to God to hear the news of your elevation. I delayed so long a time to send a messenger to your Holiness, because a certain envoy of the English King came to our venerable Archbishop of Lyons to discuss my affairs. However, he brought no acceptable proposal and having heard the Archbishop's reply on my behalf, he returned to the King, promising to come back to Lyons. I waited for his return so that I might know what I would be able to impart concerning the King's disposition – however he has not yet returned. So I now lay before you my cause, succinctly and clearly, because during my stay at Rome, I often analysed it for Pope Urban and many others, as I think your Holiness knows.

When in England, I observed many evils, the correction of which belonged to my office alone, but I could neither correct nor, without sinning, tolerate such evils. The King required of me, as if by right, that I should accede to all his wishes, but these were neither in accordance with the law of the land nor the will of God. The King forbade any recognition of the Pope or any appeal to be made in England to the Holy Father without his authority. He also instructed me not to communicate with the Pope by letter nor receive a letter from him, or obey his decrees. He allowed no Church Council to be held in his Kingdom, from the moment of his succession, for a space of, as it is now, 13 years. Lands belonging to the Church have been given to his own men. In regard to all these and similar matters I sought advice from all who held power in that Kingdom, even my own Bishops, but they refused, as if chained to his will. Accordingly, observing these and many other things which are contrary to the law of the land as well as the law of God, I begged leave of the King to pay a visit to the Holy See so that I could receive spiritual counsel and instruction with regards to my duty. The King replied that the mere making of such a request was an offence against him, and gave me the choice, either to make satisfaction to him for such a fault, pledge myself never to repeat it, promise never to appeal to the Pope, or leave his realm immediately. I chose the latter rather than commit a sin. I came to Rome and, as you know, laid the whole matter before the Pope. The King, as soon as I left his country, taxed the very victuals and clothes of our monks. He invaded the See of Canterbury and seized its revenues for his own use. Admonished and warned by Pope Urban to set this right, he treated the Pope's words with contempt and still persists in his sin. Now, it is the third year since I left England. The little money I brought with me as well as the large sums which I borrowed, of which I am still a debtor, I have now spent. So, owing more than I possess, I have sheltered in the house of our Reverend Father, the Archbishop of Lyons, being supported by his generosity and kindness. I pray therefore, and beg as earnestly as I can, that you by no means, order me to return to England, unless on such conditions as may enable me to set the law and the will of God, as well as the Apostolic Decrees above the will of man. In addition the King must restore to me the lands of the Church, as well as whatever else he has taken from the Archbishopric, or at least make compensation for what he has seized. If I acted otherwise, I would give the pretence that I preferred man to God, and that I had been justly deprived of my rank for having appealed to the Apostolic See. You can see how execrable such a precedent would be for prosperity. Some not very wise people, have asked why I do not excommunicate the King. However, those wise and better advised, counselled me not to do so, because I cannot act as both plaintiff and a judge in my own case. Moreover, some of my friends, who are subjects of the same King, have sent me messages that my excommunication, if it took place, would be despised and ridiculed by him. Naturally, with regard to all these matters, your authority and wisdom need little advice from me. I therefore pray that God Almighty may direct all your acts so they may serve His good pleasure, and that Holy Mother Church may long rejoice under your prosperous government. Amen."

I sat, half listening to a buzzing fly which came whirling through a window like some noisy imp from hell. I got down from the stool and went to the window. On the grass squatted the abbey cat, a fearsome brute whom the monks called Attila, a skilled hunter, a subtle assassin: he'd brought down a pigeon and was now watching the poor bird flutter helplessly beneath his outstretched paws. The summer did not seem so fragrant. I picked up the goblet and banged it against the stonework. Attila jumped, the pigeon broke free and still unhurt, made its escape. Attila turned to glare at me, back raised, tail curling, mouth snarling. I forced a smile as I recalled my master's teaching how every being functions according to its nature. Attila trapped and killed his food – what was wrong with that? Had I been cruel? Despite my smile, Attila glared at me and slunk away. I felt guilty and leaned against the stone wall. Nevertheless, what I had just seen was a parable about my master's situation during his exile under the Red King. In the summer of that fateful 1100, we had been truly trapped. William held us close, we were penniless, exiled, unassisted by anyone. The See of Canterbury was ransacked by the King, no money or sustenance were sent abroad. If it hadn't been for the kindness of others, Anselm could have been a beggar on the highway. Then deliverance had appeared like a comet searing through the darkest night, illuminating everything. Messengers, both royal and monastic, hurrying across the Narrow Seas to tell us that the Red King was dead!

I moved across and picked up the other document Anselm had indicated. I knew what it was, I had studied it so many times: King Henry's letter to Anselm, in exile, in which he announced his brother's death and begged Anselm to return. I paused and realised something significant: Anselm was an Archbishop of England, a Benedictine Monk, a scholar, a man revered in France, Normandy, and Italy as well as England. He had many friends; people corresponded with him secretly, but never once, for all his holiness, austerity and prayer, had Anselm any premonition that the Red King was about to die. Indeed that letter to Pope Paschal proved the point, Anselm truly believed that he could not compromise with Rufus so he would never ever return home. Was that a statement of fact or a cry of desperation? For a while I stood and turned my world upside down. Could Anselm have been part of a conspiracy? I rejected the notion. If he had, this investigation would not have ensued and yet it was a pertinent point. Anselm stood at the heart of the English Church, the leading opponent of the Red King, a dreamer, a thinker, yes even a saint in his own life time. Nevertheless, as far as I knew, he had not the slightest inkling of any danger threatening the Red King. If he had, he would have certainly told me, and perhaps even tried to warn his passionate, tempestuous, royal master. It was a thought worth saving, so where did these Benedictine monks with all their visions get their premonitions? Oh, I believe in portents, dreams and omens but not so specific, so direct, so close to the actual tragedy. I recognised this to be a fact and one to which my master would certainly return: if these rumours weren't encouraged by the Benedictine Order, their masters, or disillusioned churchmen, then by whom? I unrolled the second letter and read it.

"Henry by the grace of God, King of the English, to his most pious, virtuous, Father Anselm, Archbishop of Canterbury, health and all friendly greetings. Know dearest Father that my brother, King William, is dead and I, by the grace of God, have been chosen by the clergy and the people of England, and against my will by reason of your absence, already consecrated King. I call upon you as my Father, joining my voice to that of the entire people of England, to return here with all haste so as to extend to me and the same people of England, your care for our souls which have been committed to you. Myself and the people of the entire realm of England, commit ourselves to your guidance. I pray you are not to be displeased because I have received consecration by other hands than yours. I would have more gladly received it from you than from any other man but needs must in such a case, for my enemies desire to rise against me and the people whom I have to govern rages strong. In such an emergency therefore, I received consecration from your suffragans. I would have made to you a remittance of money by some of my courtiers, however the death of my brother has caused such a commotion throughout the dominion of England, that this could by no means have reached you safely. I therefore advise you not to travel by way of Normandy but by Wissant. I will have my barons at Dover to meet you with money so that you'll be able, by God's help, to pay what you have borrowed. Make haste, Father, to return here, for our Mother the Church of Canterbury, so long agitated and distressed on your account, can sustain no further loss of souls."

I re-read Henry's letter begging Anselm to return. The reception of my master in England was outstanding, his importance was emphasised time and again and yet the more I studied the sentences and phrases of the royal letter, the deeper my uncertainty grew. Here was Henry of England, probably a few days after his brother had been killed, writing to Anselm in France begging him to return, promising to concede everything.

Now of course, after Anselm returned, Henry withdrew many of his promises but this letter indicated something much more important. Henry realised and appreciated that his enemies were watching both here and abroad. He did not want Anselm to fall into their hands. One further fact did intrigue me. Anselm was Archbishop of Canterbury but the dangers facing Henry were so great that he advises his Archbishop to return, not through Normandy, but by some other route. He also adds the warning that he would have loved to have sent Anselm some money but felt unable to do so because of his enemies, yet this was the same Kingdom from which Walter Tirel, who had recently been the direct cause of this letter, had slipped out without any difficulty whatsoever. Henry had also been very cunning. I clearly remember that journey to Wissant, landing at Dover, the reception, the parades, the acclamation, yet as regards the relationship between King and Church, Anselm found very little had changed. Henry insisted that he expected Anselm to do homage to him in order to receive investiture of his office. Anselm retorted, and I smiled at this, if that was what King Henry wanted, he'd best return from whence he came. Henry temporised, realising that he needed Anselm's assistance. In the end Anselm had received restoration by charter of the See of Canterbury and its possessions, on the understanding that the question of his investiture and homage as Archbishop be adjourned until the following Easter, so that these matters could be discussed and the Pope's advice sought. Anselm, in the interests of peace, had accepted this.

Nevertheless, Henry's letter had been an abrupt change of fortune. I felt a chill of fear. I could follow my master's logic, the hypothesis he had fashioned, the evidence was so eloquent and compelling. Anselm's letter to the Pope described a truly dismal situation. The Red King was obdurate, he ruled both Church and realm, he would not change so Anselm would die a penniless exile. Henry's letter, however sent Fortune's Wheel whirling a full turn. Anselm was to come home immediately; he was needed desperately by both King and kingdom. The new King would listen to him; he would concede all Anselm wanted. Of course, Anselm and Henry later fought vigorously and bitterly, but that occurred later on. The conclusion was transparent: if anyone truly benefited from the Red King's death it was Anselm and, by implication, the Church. I must confess my mind drifted to the doctrine of tyrannicide advocated by the ancients and a few schoolmen, how it was a perfectly moral act to kill a despot. Had such a theory been advanced here? After all, the warnings about the Red King's death had been monkish in origin, Benedictine inspired. It's an easy step to proclaim what God wants, or to think what God wants, then move inexorably to giving God's will a helping hand. Had that happened over the death of the Red King? Anselm, of course, would not involve himself in such an act, but others in the Church? I leaned against my desk and wondered about the possibilities. Anselm, as soon as he returned to our chamber, took up that very point. He didn't say where he'd been, but kept pacing up and down as he recited the different omens, visions and portents which preceded Rufus' death.

"Why don't you ask them yourself?"

Anselm paused his pacing and stared at me.

"What do you mean?"

"We'll write to these monks, these visionaries, consult with their superiors."

Anselm laughed and shook his head. "What!" he declared, "to travel to that monastery or this, especially Gloucester? Yes," he murmured, "many of the visions originated in Gloucester or the south-west. Ah, well," he continued, "as I remarked before, even if I did that, the good brothers wouldn't change their stories. They'd simply say that God intervened to punish the Red King and the portents were warnings which he ignored. To say any different now," he added warningly, "would be very dangerous. Yes, yes," he continued, "I wonder …" He paused, fingers to his lips "…when such rumours swept the Benedictine community here and abroad, was it a natural, logical reaction to the Red King's persecution of me and the Church, or was it something more sinister? A deliberate whispering campaign spread from one monastery to another to the prepare the kingdom for the violent, sudden death of its King."

"And, if that were true," I argued, "was Tirel the appointed assassin?"

"Why not?" Anselm replied. "He is a friend of the Church, a founder of religious houses. Was he taken up, or convinced by others, about being God's anger incarnate?"

"But, Domine?"

"Yes, Eadmer."

"Who are these people?" I asked, "the Black Monks ... ?" My voice trailed off at the look in Anselm's eyes.

"Why not me?" He voiced my thoughts. "I benefited. Well, certainly immediately, indeed it would easy to argue that Tirel was my agent. After all he and his family do have close ties with Bec, the monastery at which I studied. His kin are friends of our Order. I have even entertained Walter Tirel, Lord of Poix. Moreover, Eadmer, do you recall when that envoy from the Red King visited our host, Archbishop Hugh at Lyons?"

I nodded.

"He promised to return."

"And?" I asked.

"I believe William the King might have sent Walter Tirel."

"What, has he told you that?"

"I have written to the Lord of Poix," Anselm declared wearily, "but he has yet not replied. However, let us go back to that hunting lodge when the Red King was talking to his companions just before that fatal hunt, the evening he died. Now, let me remember."

Anselm went across to my manuscript, unrolled it and found the place.

"Ah, yes, it is here." Anselm found the entry in the manuscript and, using his finger, read it out very carefully: "'Tirel was a noble knight in France, a wealthy Chatelain of Poix and Pontoise, a most powerful magnate and a man highly skilled in the use of arms. Consequently, he was one of the King's dearest friends and his constant companion everywhere.'" Anselm glanced up, waving a finger. "Eadmer, remember that! Here is a Frenchman, being described as one of the king's dearest friends and constant companions. Anyway ..." Anselm returned to the manuscripts. "'Afterwards, while they were discussing various trivial matters, and the household attendants were gathered round the King, one of the monks from Gloucester arrived and handed his Abbot's letter to the King. On hearing its contents, the King exploded with mirth and said laughingly to Tirel: "Walter, do what is right in the business you've heard" and he replied, "So I will my Lord."'" Anselm rolled up the manuscript and put it down. "So here we have Abbot Serlo's warning from Gloucester that something terrible is about to happen. The Red King then turns to Tirel and says: 'Walter, do what is right in the business you have heard.' What does that imply Eadmer?"

I stared back unable to answer.

"To me – " Anselm touched his chest, " – the King is talking about a matter over which he himself has little power or authority, something beyond his dominion. I believe Walter, Lord of Poix, was about to be sent to me, or possibly the Holy Father, on matters concerning my quarrel with William of England. He was being told to do justice in that matter."

"Why that?" I asked.

"Because it is connected with Abbot Serlo's warnings which are very clear. William has offended God by his treatment of the Church. Rufus is now telling Walter Tirel, Lord of Poix, to do something about it. It's a logical conclusion," he continued, "as I've said, Tirel was a very close companion of the king and a friend of mine, a suitable intermediary. I wonder what message he was about to bring and to whom?"

"Were the monks of St Peter Gloucester, enemies of the King?" I asked.

Anselm shook his head. "Far from it! The Red King was a munificent benefactor of their Abbey. The Abbot was Serlo of Avranches, a monk from Mont St Michel. William often visited Gloucester. He lay ill there in 1093 and gave the monastery many estates and privileges. In 1095 he compelled Thomas of York to cede St Peter's even more estates. A year later, when the rest of the English churches were being persecuted to raise money for William accepting Normandy from his brother in pawn, he issued a splendid charter in which he confirmed a number of former grants to the Abbey of St Peter made by himself and friends including Fitzhaimo. Indeed – " Anselm chewed his lip, " – if you look at the household accounts of the King, Gloucester was his favourite place. He held his last Christmas court there in 1099. No, no, Eadmer, Abbot Serlo and the monks of Gloucester were friends of the King, lavishly patronised by him. This means that their warnings must be taken seriously, but what was their origin?"

"Domine," I insisted, "why not ask the monks themselves?"

Anselm again laughed. "Serlo has gone to his reward," he remarked dryly, "and I'll never get to the truth. Perhaps the monks, when the king held his Christmas court there, witnessed its filth and lechery and realised that something dreadful was about to happen. I don't know, but it's interesting, fascinating, something to speculate about and reflect deeply on. As to the origin of all those visions and warnings," he shook his head, "God works in wondrous ways but I do believe that in this case he was given more than a helping hand." Anselm peered at me as he always did at the end of one of his homilies or a tortuous letter or document he'd dictated. "Come, Brother," he urged, "let us walk, escape these confines."

We left the chamber, locking the doors securely behind us. Brothers passed us by, they bowed to Anselm, he replied by sketching a benediction in the air. He leaned heavily on my arm.

I felt how fragile he was.

"Are you well, Father?" I urged.

He paused, gave a blessing in the direction of a group of brothers, then glanced at me.

"You know I am not, Eadmer. I am bound for God's court. I may not have many days left." He patted his stomach. "My death is upon me, but don't grieve. Don't you realise, Eadmer, all those problems I have studied: why God became man. How the Trinity is truth, man's free will and God's grace, will all be resolved. I will spend eternity absorbing the truth, but for the moment, there's this matter. We must concentrate on that and only that."

We continued along the stone passageways. Anselm stopped now and again to savour the different smells, the sweet odours from the kitchen, the incense smoke wafting from the church, the delicious fragrance, as Anselm put it, from the writing carrels. "Ravishing," he exclaimed, "manuscripts freshly scrubbed, ink turned from powder."

We left the Abbey and moved into the orchards. Anselm joked that heaven would be like this, greenery all about us, fresh grass shooting up, long and lush in the cool, dappled darkness. We walked deeper into the shade. Anselm paused as a shadow slipped through the grass – Attila was hunting again. I confessed to my earlier confrontation with the cat and jokingly asked for absolution which Anselm merrily gave. We talked a while about the possibility of pets being in heaven until we reached a glade, cool and shadowed. Anselm sat down on a log wiping the sweat from his face. I realised he was truly ill. He was pale-faced, fighting for breath. Nevertheless, when I moved towards him, he gestured me away.

"Don't talk," he whispered, "don't mention it. It's passing, it will go." He gazed around the greenery and for a while we played a game much loved by my master: the labelling of flowers. We identified foxglove with its tooth leaves, small toadflax with its grey-violet colouring, the bright red berries of bitter-sweet, woody nightshade, the blue-green of grey meadow rue now dying as summer reached its fullness. Afterwards we went searching for a holm oak in the woods beyond. Anselm remarked how this was his favourite tree. We found one and Anselm smoothed the grey-brown bark with his hand.

"Sturdy and reliable," he laughed, "one of the few constants in life."

We returned to the glade. Anselm sat on a log staring up through the interlaced branches.

"It's good to be here," he murmured, "refreshing to escape from it all, but we must resolve this."

"What, Father?"

"An unlawful death, Eadmer," he whispered, "that's what we are dealing with. When we are finished today – " he winked at me, " – forget the Divina Lectio – the Divine Office. I instruct you, turn your mind to this matter. Ah, well," he continued, "the sun is beginning to fade and the day's work will soon be done. You must wonder where I went when I left our chamber. Well, Eadmer, we have a visitor, he must now be settled as I am, having taken the air!"

"Master, I apologise. I've asked this before, but where is this all leading?"

"I told you, Brother – " he smiled up at me, " – I want to know the truth about the Red King's death!"

"What does it matter, Father, he is long dead?"

"The truth matters, Eadmer, particularly if I'm involved. I'm Archbishop of Canterbury, I was the guardian of that King's soul. I have responsibilities. I must know the truth. I want also to confess something, Brother. I believe I was involved in his death."

I stared back in astonishment.

"Oh, yes, Brother." Anselm pointed a finger at me. "I believe I was involved in his death, not voluntarily, not 'sua sponte' – on my own accord, but I was involved, so therefore, I must know the truth. I have a duty to discharge." He wetted his lips and stared around the glade. "Every day I pray for poor William's soul. It is not only because I am Archbishop of Canterbury, Chaplain to the King, or because of logic or truth. There's something else." He leaned forward, hands together. "Eadmer, I truly loved William son of the Conqueror. Oh," he paused, "undoubtedly opposites attract each other. He was loud-mouthed, aggressive, violent, secular, pagan, lecherous, indulging in sin but, at the same time …"

"Yes, Master."

"He was human." Anselm smiled at me. "All of Europe, Eadmer, congratulates me on my work: *Cur Deus Homo* – 'Why God became Man'. As I have said, Christ became man not to make us Christian, but to make us fully human. He became man not just to save us from our sins, but to experience what we experience. To stand on a shore, to feel the breeze, go fishing, flirt with a woman, be thirsty, eat, feast. For all his faults, William the Red King certainly did that, he lived life to the full. There was no hypocrisy in him, Brother. He didn't say one thing and act another. What you saw was the truth. He cursed, he fornicated, he hunted, he spat, he drank and got drunk, but in the end, he was truly nothing more than a child. He loved the things of this world. I have studied the Old Testament. I am fascinated by another King, David. Now there's a man who loved wine, a beautiful face, soft flesh, perfume, luxury, opulence and yet he was a beautiful poet, a musician. He wasn't an ascetic, an archbishop," he laughed dryly, "or a monk, or a preacher. David was a King, yet God describes him, remember this Eadmer, as 'a man after my own heart'. William the Red King could have been that. I truly believe, Brother, he had goodness in him, an honesty which God will recognise. Consequently, it is not only that I'm Archbishop of Canterbury or that I owe a debt, but as his friend, I want to seek the truth, and in a way – " he blinked as his eyes welled with tears, " – I want to purge my own sin. Yes, yes," he murmured as if talking to himself, "I need to seek his absolution for not resolving this earlier. Come Eadmer, our visitor! He must now be refreshed and replenished, let's visit him."

He made to rise, but then sat down again with a sigh, put his face in his hands and began to sob gently. I crouched down and pulled his hands apart. He stared tearfully at me. "Did you read those letters, Brother?"

"Of course I did."

"And did you reflect on how similar they are? Do you realise, Brother, my letter may have started it all?"

I gazed back in puzzlement.

"My letter to Pope Paschal." Anselm grasped my hands. "It was a final, absolute statement; the Pope had to act to save the Church in England. My letter must have become common knowledge – Henry virtually answered it clause by clause. It must have been known to my brother Benedictines – hence the visions and the portents. Above all, it must have been known to the Red King."

"And?"

"Was he going to make peace? Was Tirel to be used to, and I quote, 'obtain justice in that matter.'" Anselm sighed. "Whatever, that letter and, I believe, Duke Robert's imminent return were the catalyst of what later happened. Ah well – " he let go of my hands and stood up, " – it is not yet finished!"

V

Sext

Historical Notes

The two letters mentioned here can be found in Schmitt's edition (Epp [Letters], 210 and 212) and Eadmer, *Historia Novorum in Anglia* (op. cit.), p.124. The significance of both these letters will be discussed in a later section. One fact which does emerge is Anselm's fondness for the Red King: he could have roused Europe against him, demanded excommunication, conspired with others. He never did. I believe Eadmer: Anselm's tears, his grief at the news of the Red King's death were genuine.

VI

Nones

Release me from the snares they have hidden.
(Psalm 30)

We returned to the Abbey, where I thought my master would go directly to the refectory but instead we turned into the church.

"I have loved, Oh Lord," he intoned, as we entered through the main door, "the beauty of Thy house and the place where Thy glory dwells. For a day with You is better than a thousand elsewhere."

We crossed ourselves, genuflected and went up the cool, glorious nave resplendent in its splendid columns and shifting light, rich with the perfume of beeswax, incense and flowers. We turned into one of the darkened transepts and entered the Lady Chapel, a beautiful hallowed place, the candles flaming beneath the statue of the Virgin Mary, crowned as a Queen, holding the Divine Infant on her lap. We knelt on the prie-dieu before the shrine and Anselm intoned one of his favourite prayers.

"Hail Mary, full of Grace, you are the glory of our race …"

Once finished we went out through the stone-hollowed galleries to the far side of the abbey and the two-storey guest house, a grey, ragstone building fronting a small courtyard. Ivo and Reginald, the Archbishop's messengers, lounged on a bench outside, flicking dried peas into a nearby horse trough. They rose and bowed as my master approached.

"Domine." Ivo's mischievous face broke into a smile. "He's inside, well fed and refreshed, but he still insists on eating."

Anselm sketched a blessing in their direction, entered the small vestibule turning left into the refectory with its lime-washed walls, the raftered beams draped in coloured cloths displaying the five wounds of Christ. At the far end, a stark black cross was nailed to the wall. The floor was scrubbed clean and covered thickly with freshly cut reeds from one of the abbey's stew ponds. Two trestle tables with benches ran either side of the refectory. The room was empty except for a man sitting beneath the window at the top of the far table. He was dressed in dirt-stained homespun, a tangled moustache and beard hid his lower face whilst his bushy, greying hair was tied back behind his head. A broad, thick-set man, with watery blue eyes in a weather-chaffed face, he stared at us then returned to attacking the food heaped on a platter before him: chicken flesh, dried ham and a vegetable potage. He only stopped eating to grasp the leather tankard, slurp noisily, belch, then grin at us. He half-rose as Anselm crossed the refectory towards him, but as if the food was too tempting, slumped back on the stool quickly pushing food into his mouth as if he feared we were coming to take it from him.

"This is Purkell." Anselm sat down on the bench.

Purkell kept on eating, though he smiled, mouth gaping, his strong white teeth covered with shards of food. I heard a sound and turned. Oderic and another lay-brother slipped into the refectory and joined us at the table. The second lay-brother introduced himself as Waltheof. He looked so much like Oderic, I wondered if they were blood kin, until I gathered from Oderic's introduction that Waltheof was Saxon. He, too, had fought at Senlac in the fyrd on the right flank of the 'Fighting Man', the Wessex battle standard. They were now close friends, united by the Benedictine rule as well as memories of a common battle. Oderic assured Anselm that everything was ready. My master nodded and turned to Waltheof.

"Speak to Purkell," he said, "tell him why he is here, what I told you earlier. My messengers would have instructed him but I want to make it very clear why I must speak to him."

Waltheof spoke, the guttural Saxon echoing around the refectory. Purkell stopped eating, pushed away the platter and would have knelt at Anselm's feet, but my master laughed, made a swift blessing over the food and asked the man to continue feasting. Purkell certainly did, though listening carefully to everything Waltheof said. Up close I could see Purkell's fingers and hands were ingrained with black dirt, his clothes were holed and scorched and he gave off the pungent smell of wood-smoke. I quickly gathered that he was a charcoal burner from the New Forest and brought here by the Archbishop's messengers who'd promised him a good meal, a feast in fact, as well as some silver coins. Purkell finished his meal, drained the tankard and replied to Waltheof.

He appeared unabashed by the company or his surroundings, a man who'd told his tale many a time. He was a cottar, a freeman, holding by ancient right a plot of land on the outskirts of the New Forest, a charcoal burner working for a local manor. He knew all about the royal hunt during the grease-season, so he kept well away from the hunting paths and glades. On that particular day, he was more than aware of horsemen, horns blowing, verderers and foresters fanning out with their dogs. Purkell had known for some time that the Red King would hunt there. Late that evening the crisis broke. Something had gone wrong, horsemen galloping away, verderers and foresters clustering together talking to each other. Just before sunset a servant wearing the royal livery came to his cottage and demanded that he hitch up his cart and bring it immediately to a nearby glade. Purkell declared this wasn't too surprising. Local carts were often requisitioned to bring back game from the hunt, so the charcoal burner did as asked, helped by his younger brother. He knew the glade was nearby. He'd often been there and he remembered a small church, a hermitage had also stood there before the forestation of the area. He hitched his cart and led it onto a trackway leading into the glade. Men were running about. Nobles on horseback were already leaving the forest, heading for the Roman road leading north-east to Winchester. In the clearing beneath the outstretched branches of an oak tree, squatted some royal retainers. They were staring helplessly at a man lying on the ground, the front of his rich tunic stained with blood. Purkell talked evenly as if he was describing the felling of a deer. He led the cart across. Somebody whispered it was the King. He and his brother wrapped the corpse in its cloak, laid it in on the cart and brought it into Winchester.

"And that was it?" I asked Waltheof. He in turn, translated my question. Purkell just shrugged, picked up a chicken bone and gnawed greedily at the remaining shards of meat. He glanced across and spoke quickly.

Waltheof smiled at me. "There was little ceremony," he translated, "nothing to distinguish that King from a piece of meat lying on a trestle. He picked him up as he would the carcass of a deer, wrapped the cloak about, put it on the cart and left the forest taking the road to Winchester."

"No, no!" Anselm intervened, jabbing a finger at Waltheof. "Tell him to describe exactly what he saw in the glade."

Waltheof translated. Purkell raised his eyes in astonishment, licked his fingers, spread his hands and spoke so quickly Waltheof told him to slow down. Eventually we made sense of it. Apparently the King was lying there. He had a green tunic on with blue leggings beneath. Purkell remembered the costly leather boots, the silver-gilt spurs. He also had a belt round his waist. The long, embroidered cloak around him had been hitched up. Nearby lay a bow, its string broken, next to it a quiver of arrows. From the King's chest protruded a broken shaft which pierced his chest, Purkell pointed to his left side, close to the heart. Blood crusted his lips and trickled through his nose. The King's clothes were covered in dust, his face pale.

"And the shaft?" Anselm asked. "You are sure it was broken?"

"From what I gather," Waltheof translated, "the King had been struck by an arrow, broken the shaft off, then fell on it. The body had been turned over." Purkell gabbled on, chattering like a jay. Anselm asked Waltheof what he had said.

"He was concerned," the lay-brother replied. "By then no Great Ones milled about, no horsemen anywhere. They'd all gone."

"And then what happened?" Anselm asked.

Waltheof translated. Purkell put down what he was eating, leaned against the table and talked so fast Waltheof again had to tell him to slow down so he could translate. Apparently the King's body was lowered onto the cart, still covered in his cloak. Purkell followed at the tail – his brother leading the horse. They needed little encouragement, being offered a half mark of silver between them for their work.

"Was the corpse accompanied?" Anselm asked.

Purkell shook his head. "Some of the mercenaries from the Royal Hunting Lodge, valets of the chamber." From the way he narrowed his eyes, I could see Purkell was referring to some of the less desirables who thronged the Red King's Court. "They followed, some were crying, others were shouting curses."

"And the man who killed the King?" Anselm asked.

Purkell pulled a face and shook his head. "No sight of him, though I gather from those who followed the corpse, that if they'd laid their hands on him they would have done him hurt."

"And no Great Ones of the land. You are sure?" Anselm insisted.

Again with a shake of the head, Purkell continued his description, how blood had seeped through the Red King's cloak, dripping onto the cart. They reached the gates of Winchester just before dawn. They were allowed in, and went through the cobbled streets into the square before the Old Minster. There, the corpse had been met by monks led by their Prior Godfrey of Cambrai, a poet whom I knew. Purkell, chattering on, explained how the corpse was taken into the death house and later in the morning, with some of the Great Ones in attendance, buried under the Old Tower of the Minster Church …

Anselm then intervened, gesturing for Purkell to be silent. I could see my master was disturbed by something. Beads of sweat had appeared on his brow. He'd grown more agitated. I wondered why but I dare not ask the reason in the presence of others. The questioning continued. Purkell replied that he and the others had stayed outside the church but yes, the burial had taken place fairly quickly. Anselm drew the matter to a close, reassuring Purkell that he'd done well, promising him a soft bed, a few coins of silver and a safe journey back to the New Forest.

Anselm then left the guest house, went outside and stood for a while in the courtyard staring up at the sky. It was a beautiful evening, the sun slowly setting. My master turned, he looked ill and old, the dark rings under his eyes seemed deeper. He looked beyond me. Oderic and Waltheof were standing in the doorway.

"Make sure poor Purkell is looked after," he said, "then we will do it."

A short while later we left the Abbey buildings and walked down into the great meadow. This time we went through it, across the wooden bridge over the stream and into the woods beyond. Oderic and Waltheof followed. Crude wooden shields had been hung from the branches of trees, each painted with a different colour. Oderic and Waltheof produced their bows and quivers of arrows, slinging them over their shoulder, talking and joking between themselves. Anselm remained strangely quiet. He then beckoned me over and we walked away from the bowmen. I stood and watched. Waltheof and Oderic were talking to each other as we separated. They took up position, bows stretched, the cords hummed and the arrows whirred like the sound of bird wings before the shafts hit their mark. This continued for some time.

Once they'd finished Anselm called both lay-brothers over to him and we all walked across to the different shields.

"Well, Master," I asked, "what were you trying to prove?"

"Look at the different targets," Anselm said. "Come, Eadmer, can you tell me which of the arrows embedded here are from Oderic's bow and which are from Waltheof's?"

Of course I couldn't and confessed as much. Anselm nodded.

"But if I told you," he said, "that the grey flights belong to Oderic and the black to Waltheof, you'd know then wouldn't you?"

I agreed. We walked away. The two lay-brothers remained on the other side of the glade talking busily between themselves. I glanced around that dark, green place, the lush grass, the old trees, their branches interlacing, birdsong, soft noises rattling the dense, tangled undergrowth. I recalled Purkell's description and thought this is how it must have been on that fateful evening, when a king lay mysteriously slain in a glade, an arrow shaft embedded deep in his chest.

"What are you trying to prove, Master?"

"Something very simple." Anselm peered at me. "Eadmer, people are so certain that Walter Tirel loosed that killing arrow at the King but how do they know? Oderic, Waltheof," he shouted, "come over here!" Both swaggered over as if they were reverting to their warrior days, quivers slapping against their side, powerful bows in their hands.

"Separate," Anselm ordered. "Separate, and loose arrows."

They did so – again the glade was broken by the thrum of the bow, the whirr of the arrows, the smack as they hit their target. Anselm told them to do it faster. As they did so he instructed me to watch most carefully who loosed which arrow. Of course, I couldn't and said so. At last, Anselm clapped his hands, thanked the brothers and dismissed them. He took me over to a rocky outcrop, and sat down on the moss-soaked stone staring at the back of his hands.

"What I am trying to say, Brother – " Anselm lifted his head, " – is this. Everyone is so certain that Walter Tirel killed the King, yet how do they know that? Who saw it? Who can go on oath and swear they saw a certain arrow loosed from a certain bow at a certain time strike the King. To do that you'd have to watch the archer, then the flight of the arrow until it hits its target. Now the only way you could do that is if you are waiting for something to happen, but this was supposed to be an accident, so how do people know it was Tirel's arrow which struck the King? There is only one conclusion, Eadmer," he continued, "the arrow which struck the King must have been one held by Walter Tirel, true? Which takes us back to that conversation at the hunting lodge at Brockenhurst? Do you remember? The King was presented with six beautiful arrows. He kept four for himself and gave two to Tirel, saying it was only appropriate that sharpest arrows should be given to the deadliest archer. Consequently, people must have recognised one of those arrows which struck the Red King. Rufus had four, Tirel two, therefore, it must have come from Tirel." Anselm paused as if listening to the chatter of the birds above him. "When we study the events of the Red King's reign, we deal with Flambard, a veritable rogue," he added, "steeped in villainy. Very interesting! People maintain Flambard's mother was a witch, as you do in your account. Anyway, I've heard stories, rumours, that Rufus' death was not murder, not an accident, but actually suicide."

"Master!" I gasped.

"Oh, yes," Anselm pressed on, "a theory that Rufus was not really a Christian, but belonged to the old religion of ancient rites, that he offered himself as a victim and that Tirel was the priest who carried this out."

I stared at my master, then burst out laughing. Anselm joined in.

"Precisely, my dear secretary," he said, "you'd have to possess a mind as nimble as a scribe's pen to follow that argument.

However – " he waved a hand, " – it has been said that the Red King somehow was offering himself as a royal sacrifice. To whom, or for what, I don't know." He sighed deeply and rose to his feet. "It just shows you, Eadmer, how silly people can become, yet I learnt a lot tonight. Look – " he patted me on the shoulder, " – you go back to our chamber, say a prayer, prepare yourself for sleep."

"Why Master, where are you going?"

"I want to talk to Purkell again, not to mention our infirmarian."

"Master, are you sick?"

"Eadmer, you know I am. Whilst there's nothing under God's heaven that can cure me, I will be with you shortly."

I returned to our chamber alone. Sometimes my master slept in the same chamber as I. Other times, I know, he went back into the church to prostrate himself on the cold paving stones before the Pyx to pray. Occasionally he'd go out into the cold night, turning some problem over in his mind in a ruthless search for a solution.

The sun was setting. I decided to stay up a bit longer and joined the good brothers in church. Anselm said I was excused from reciting the Divine Office but, when I could, I was determined to remain as much as possible within the horarium of the abbey. I went down into the nave of the church and knelt on a prie-dieu, staring up at a coloured cloth depicting the Passion of Christ, the heart circled with thorns, the hands and feet pierced by nails, the side opened by a spear. I stared hard, trying to meditate, free from distractions, yet they came, thick and fast. I gasped and sprang to my feet, hands to my face. The sacred painting recalled what the charcoal burner had said, how blood had seeped from the corpse, dripping through the cloak onto the cart as it was taken into Winchester. Even I, with my lack of medical knowledge, know full well that, when a man is dead, the blood ceases to flow, there's no rhythm or beat of life in the wrist or neck. So, if blood was still dripping from Rufus' corpse, splashing out, had the King been killed outright or had he been mortally wounded and died on his way to Winchester? If that was the case, how could anyone believe stories about the Red King's corpse being surrounded by nobles grieving and lamenting over his death? If Purkell was correct, William had been struck by a shaft to the heart. He snapped off the shaft, and fell to the ground, but if his body had been dripping blood, still oozing out as he was carried to Winchester, that means the King was not truly dead. So what care had been taken over him? Did that concern my master? What was he really trying to prove? Father Anselm was deeply troubled and agitated. I decided to go in search of my master and found him sitting in the great cloister garth, Attila acting all coy, resting in his lap. Anselm was stroking the cat absent-mindedly, lips moving as if talking to that unseen presence. He glanced up as I approached.

"Master, the blood from that corpse?"

"I know, I know," he replied, holding up his hand, "but leave that for a while Eadmer. I want you to carefully meditate on all you have written and learnt." Then he would say no more.

* * *

Over the next two days, more messengers arrived, bringing urgent letters for Anselm. At the time I never discovered the reason why. According to gossip, on one occasion Anselm was found seated in the small garden next to the kitchen, crying quietly into his hands. A lay-brother reported this to me. However, when I went to visit him, Anselm was dry-eyed and rather sharp, and refused to discuss the matter. Instead, he again asked me to reflect on what I had read, written and learnt over the last few days whilst we both prepared for the arrival of the King and his other guests. In fact the good brothers regarded this as one of the most important events of the year. Paths were cleared, gardens tended to, supplies off-loaded from great carts in the kitchen-yard: beer, ale, wine, venison, cider, fresh meat, chickens, geese and hare. The church was scoured and cleaned and everything made ready, though Anselm kept apart from this. I only met him once in the cloister garden. Anselm was sitting on a stone ledge peering at an ant crawling across his hand.

"You know what I want, Eadmer?" He glanced up at me. "Just think about what happened. Perhaps put down your thoughts summarising events?"

I did so and was surprised at how a story I'd accepted as a fact, that the Red King had been killed in a hunting accident in the New Forest was very much open to question – but the truth? Perhaps that was my fear, that my master was wasting his time following a path leading nowhere. Perhaps there were no answers to the questions I posed. However, on that sunny Lammas Day 1st August 1108, I duly followed my master's instruction, sitting in our chamber reflecting on everything I'd learnt about the death of the Red King.

Primo: The Red King had definitely been killed on the evening of 2nd August whilst hunting in the New Forest but why did he go hunting so late? What was the real delay? Why not earlier? Why didn't he wait until the next day?

Secundo: Had he been killed outright? The more I thought about Purkell's report the more curious I became. I'm no physician. I know very little about the treatment of wounds or the disturbance of the humours, so I made my way down to the infirmary and talked to Brother Theodore, a man skilled in the use of herbs, poultices, potions and powders. He had seen service in God's army in Outremer, fought under the boiling hot sun in Palestine and even picked up medical knowledge from his opponents, the scholars and holy men of Islam. I told him exactly what had happened. Theodore, keen as a bird, listened attentively; now and again he'd lift a darkened hand and scratch a spot on his cheek, then return to peering at the wall, head slightly cocked, listening to my every word. Occasionally he'd point a bony finger and ask me to repeat what I had said. I became quite tired but at last Theodore was satisfied in establishing what he called 'the symptoms'.

"You see, Brother Eadmer." Theodore straightened up in his chair playing with the apron band round his waist. "When the body dies, the heart is stopped, the blood ceases to flow. We don't understand the motions of the humours or the reason why blood should flow or how it flows, suffice to say it's the life force of the body. If you lose too much you die, and that is the problem: the blood is moved by the humours of the emotions, when those emotions cease the blood stops flowing. No blood beat can be detected in neck or wrist. So, to answer your question, if blood was still seeping from the King's wound then I would question whether he was dead or not."

"But an arrow to the heart?" I asked.

"Not necessarily." He shook his head. "It does not bring instant death, as I said, it is when the blood flow stops that death ensues."

"Are you saying, Brother Theodore, and I must caution you to secrecy, that the Red King may have been still alive?"

He raised his eyebrows, pursed his lips and nodded vigorously.

"Of course, it's not unknown. Men have received arrows to the heart, to the neck, to the throat, the belly, to all intents and purposes they are unconscious, dying, some may even think they're dead, but if blood is flowing so copiously from a wound, then I doubt if death has ensued."

I thanked the infirmarian and left. I walked for a while in the cloister garden. I went across to the lavarium, the small channel of running water where the monks washed their hands. I cleaned mine carefully. I watched the water drip into a pot beneath and thought of the King's blood sopping out, staining the cart. If that occurred had those around him taken care of the King? Was any medical assistance given? Even I, who have attended the dead, have seen people search for the life beat at the throat or wrist, people putting their ear to the chest, listening intently, holding a mirror to the lips to catch the breath that had apparently not happened to the Red King, which led to my third question. I returned to my studies in our chamber.

Tertio: The Red King was not excommunicated, yet by his life, he'd openly rejected the teaching of the Church. Indeed, according to many ecclesiastics, he had plundered the Holy Mother Church of its possessions, driven its leader Archbishop Anselm into exile, therefore he had been struck down by God. Nevertheless, hadn't anyone thought of sending for a priest, so that his last few minutes could be hallowed, absolution offered, a blessing made? Surely there were chapels around, and hadn't monks visited the Royal Hunting Lodge at Brockenhurst? Indeed no physical or spiritual consolation appears to have been offered to the fallen King.

Quarto: Had the King been shouting at somebody just before he was struck? Telling them to loose, to shoot at 'the devil'? Was that because the King's bow string had snapped. If it did, had that any significance?

Quinto: Walter Tirel – how did people know that he was the man responsible? Did someone see him? And afterwards, how did a Frenchman, a stranger to this realm, manage to find his way so easily to the coast and take ship to France, no hindrance or obstacle being offered? True, I could understand people feeling sorry for him or trying to protect him from the King's immediate retainers, yet he could have been guarded, questioned later to establish exactly what had happened.

Sexto: Was it simply an accident? The timing, the place, the means? Did those around respond as if it were mere mischance?

Septimo: If it wasn't an accident, then it was murder. If so, who profited? Walter Tirel, according to the evidence, had immediately left the spot and returned to France without any obvious gain. The Great Lords later supported Henry but they had been the Red King's most ardent adherents and there was no evidence of any rift or difference between them and Rufus. Why should they kill a Royal Master who patronised them so favourably? Was it fratricide? Had Prince Henry decided to kill his own brother, but if that was the case, surely the Great Lords would not support a man who'd kill his brother like Cain killed Abel, and why should they? Had it been murder by someone else, a stranger with a grievance which has never come to light? However, that would take considerable organisation and planning. Anyone entering that royal forest risked being taken by verderers, huntsmen or royal guards. Surely there'd have been occasions more suitable, more appropriate?

Octavo: All those omens and portents, what was their significance? Was it just that people held their breath as they watched the Red King plunder the Church, keep bishoprics and abbacies empty, exile Anselm and openly ridicule the Pope? Did they see Rufus' sudden and violent death merely as a logical conclusion, something they could anticipate. Were the omens and visions the ripe fruit of hindsight? Or had it been something else? My master was correct. All those portents and omens seem to originate from the south-west, whether it was Gloucester or Cornwall. What was particular about that? My master was perceptive. The Black Monks of St Benedict had a great deal to answer for. Monks at Gloucester had dreams and visions whilst even their brothers in France seemed to mysteriously learn what was to happen, or had happened. Guess work, hindsight or something more sinister?

Nono: Why was my master so agitated, so deeply involved in this matter? True, he was Archbishop of Canterbury, he believed he had a duty, a loyalty to the dead King whose care had been entrusted to him by Lanfranc. Did my master know something which he had not shared with me? Why had he invited King Henry, his brother Robert, the Queen and those leading courtiers to this abbey? Anselm had given the excuse that his days were drawing to an end and that he wished to make his farewells. Nevertheless, I had this feeling that Anselm, with his logical ways, sharp mind and keen wits, believed he had certain business to finish before he rendered his final account.

Decimo: Those two letters: Anselm's to the Pope and Henry's to my master? Anselm was right. Henry must have seen a copy for he virtually answers every point Anselm raised with the Pope, be it the rights of the Church or the question of reparation, even down to paying my master's debts. Anselm's letter to Pope Paschal amounted to a stark declaration of war between Church and State, as well as a grim description of Anselm's personal circumstances. The letter must have been circulated amongst the Benedictine community which included Gloucester. Is that what prompted those dreams and visions? Moreover, if Henry had seen a copy, so must the Red King. Is that what he was referring to immediately after he'd received Abbot Serlo's warning? He'd turned to Tirel and asked him 'to do justice in the matter'. Was Tirel being sent to Rome to put the King's case? If that was true, then the Red King's death took on a different hue. Was he killed to stop this and was Tirel depicted as the slayer, albeit accidentally, to discredit him?

VI

Nones
Historical Notes

I admit Purkell's role, (or in other accounts Purkiss) is a later addition. A variety of narratives describe how Rufus' corpse was transported to Winchester though the accounts of the corpse dripping blood are fairly clear as is the fact that it was given hasty and rather undignified burial, Oderic Vitalis (op. cit.), p.292. Rufus' tomb at Winchester, amongst others, was disturbed by Cromwell's men. The alleged tomb was opened a number of times and, on one occasion, the fragments of a wooden shaft and iron arrow-head were found. If this was true, it emphasises how Rufus' corpse, ill-tended and unprepared, was hastily bundled into its grave. The debate about the tomb, however, has yet to be resolved: J. Crook 'The Rufus Tomb in Winchester Cathedral', *The Antiquaries Journal*, Vol. 79, (1999), pp.187-212. The theory that the Red King was the victim of some ancient rite is discussed by M.A. Murray, *The Divine King in England* (Faber, 1954), p.56 et seq. is interesting but scarcely believable! The question of Tirel and his arrows will be discussed later.

VII

Vespers

*You need not fear the terrors of the night
or the arrow which flies in the sunlight.*
(Psalm 91)

The day after Lammas, my master and I rose early, celebrating our Masses in the side chapel of the abbey church, then we made ready for the royal arrival. Messengers were already thundering at the gates announcing that the King and Queen were only a few miles away and would shortly arrive. They did so just after the Chapter Mass. The main gates of St Augustine's were thrown back. Anselm and leading monks of the abbey, its Chancellor, Prior, the Keeper of the Galilee Chapel and the Master of the Infirmary, gathered in the broad cloister yard clad in their best black robes. They were preceded by a cross-bearer, flanked by two acolytes carrying burning candles with a thurifer alongside them scenting the air with the sweetest incense. A beautiful summer's morning. Swallows dipped and twisted across the blue sky. From the dovecotes came a melodious cooing. Occasionally once of these brilliant white birds would swoop over the courtyard, only to flee as the hawks, peregrines and falcons on the wrists of their noble owners stirred beneath their hoods and moved angrily, setting the jesse bells tingling: a sombre warning to the doves and any other birds that the King was here to hunt as well as feast and be entertained by my master. A small choir chanted 'Honor,

Gloria et Laus tibi', their singing almost drowned by the clatter of a mass of mounted men in mailed hauberks, dark-blue leggings, stained leather boots firm in the stirrups, their faces and heads almost hidden by the Norman cone-shaped helmets with their broad nose guards. Each man held an oval-shaped shield and a long wicked-looking spear. They cantered into the yard, reeking of sweat, blood, leather and horse dung. At last the singing stopped. The mailed escort broke apart as grooms and others hurried to assist those behind. The royal party dismounted and made their way towards Archbishop Anselm who with a white stole around his neck, raised his right hand in blessing, his archiepiscopal ring winking in the sunlight. At first, as the kiss of peace was exchanged, it was hard to distinguish individuals as they milled backwards and forwards, ready to genuflect, only to pause as Anselm excused them, laughingly saying that this was no time for rites and ceremony: they were his most welcome guests and he was so pleased that they had come. Queen Mathilda stood out from the rest: a snow-white veil covered her head, framing her lovely face, its wraps going round her neck to fall behind her. She was clothed in a dark-blue cloak, a dress of deep murrey beneath, fringed with gold thread at hem and neck. Silver bracelets and precious rings shimmered on her wrists and fingers. I was standing far behind Anselm, but even from where I stood I could smell her fragrant perfume. I was truly captivated by that face, as I always was, perfect in every way, oval-shaped, her glorious golden hair was hidden by the veil, but her violet-coloured eyes sparkled with zest, that lovely mouth, her red lips parted. She smiled brilliantly at my master and grasped his hands, almost as if he was her lover rather than her spiritual father. Beside Mathilda stood the King, small and wiry, his muscular frame clothed in a white linen shirt under a red and gold tunic braided at the neck, the three-quarter length sleeves boasting silver tassels and on his thick legs, green braies, tied close with grey linen bands and on his feet thick leather shoes, high fitting to the ankle with heavy spurs clinking on the hardened heels. Henry was not red-faced like his brothers but rather dark, olive-skinned, his deep-set eyes hard as black pebbles; thin lips above an aggressive chin, the cleanly-shaved face slightly pock-marked. In deference to Father Anselm, he and his companions had shaved their heads in the old Norman fashion at both the back and sides, the rest brushed forward to their brow as if they were men who constantly donned war helmets and had no need for the fashions of the Red King's Court. Henry's hair was black and matted, it made him look what he was, aggressive but controlled, a man of few words who could be utterly charming even as he plotted your destruction. Nevertheless, he was a true king, a powerful prince who'd crushed his enemies, established peace in the Church and enforced the law throughout his dominions. Anselm deeply respected him. Henry returned the compliment though they were very wary of each other and no more so than that morning. They kissed each others rings. Henry gave me that sly lop-sided smile of his and then the other guests milled around. I had met them all before: the King's councillors, his leading retainers, the men who advised him in his secret chamber. Henry the King did not like ostentation, no brooches, or frippery, and his companions were similarly attired. Powerful men visiting friends on a warm summer's day, they had no need of ornament.

Behind the King stood Duke Robert, his reddish hair all greasy. He was ruddy faced, his cheeks vein-streaked by too much wine. His snub nose sniffed the air like a mischievous hunting dog, his protuberant merry mouth twisted into that easy smile, watery, blue eyes ever shifting as if he found all around him very amusing. Duke Robert certainly did not look like his brother's prisoner or even enforced house guest. He winked at me, bowed at Anselm and sauntered off to talk to one of the grooms. Duke Robert was a small, jovial man who had lost everything. It was hard to imagine this same person was the great Conqueror's eldest surviving son, once Duke of Normandy, a knight sworn to the

Cross, who'd fought most strenuously against the infidels and walked the streets of Holy Jerusalem. He had returned from Outremer a champion, given a rapturous welcome by many of the Great Ones of Normandy yet he had frittered everything away, finally losing all at the Battle of Tinchebrai two years earlier. Now wifeless, childless and duchyless, Robert was nothing more than an enforced guest at his brother's court. The 'Great Three' were also there – King Henry's alter egos: Fitzhaimo, the terror of the Welsh, his ghost-like face, thin, pallid, and deeply furrowed, with slanted green eyes and that strange mop of striking red hair, an angular figure, a ruthless fighter to the bone. Next to him, Robert de Beaumont, Count of Meulan, slim and slender as a sapling despite his years, his lean face like that of an ascetic under his thinning snow-white hair. Robert of Meulan with his clever, dark eyes, beaked nose and sardonic mouth, cunning as a viper and just as dangerous. A veteran of Senlac who has prospered like the cedar of Lebanon stretching in every direction, under whose shade many men sheltered. Alongside him his shadow, his brother, Henry of Warwick, lean as a greyhound, sinewy as a whippet, with his pleasant smiling face rather blotchy and pockmarked, redeemed by the strangest blue eyes which would stare unblinkingly at you.

Ah, yes, they were all assembled. Once the courtesies and protocols were over, Anselm led his guests, including me, into a small private garden of the abbey with its tinkling fountain, raised flower beds, herbaceous borders, turf seats, its sturdy trellises fashioned out of black oak, with roses of every hue climbing and curling around them. We made ourselves comfortable in the shade of a clump of pear trees, their fruit ripening to fullness above our heads. Lay-brothers served us white, chilled wine and dishes of sticky marchpane. For a while the conversation was on general matters, about the King's journey from London, what he intended to do in the New Forest, the prospect of a good harvest as well as the usual enquiries about each other's health. Queen Mathilda sat like a disciple before her master, hands in her lap staring adoringly at Anselm. Henry was uneasy, he kept moving his head, and looking around as if searching for someone. Duke Robert helped himself to the wine and, in a few minutes, downed at least two cups. The Beaumont brothers, sitting on a turf seat to the King's right, watched Anselm intently, whilst Fitzhaimo, whispering under his breath, wandered off to study what he called 'a curious herb'. In truth, they were all nervous and highly curious about my master's invitation to them. He described the events of the day. They would meet the leading monks from the abbey, eat and drink, take their rest in the afternoon and gather in the Prior's refectory or parlour for a sumptuous feast. Duke Robert declared it all a pleasant prospect and for a while he tipsily entertained us with stories about his journey to Outremer, the sea voyages and the battles he'd been involved in. The Royal Party half-listened, distracted by Anselm who sat quietly throughout. Only when the first excitement of the meeting subsided did King Henry cough, clear his throat and, hands on his knees, lean forward to catch Anselm's attention.

"Reverend Father," he began, "you have invited us here. You say your health is not good and you wish to make your farewells. However, our reply to that is may you live 'ad multos annos' – may you see many more summers as well as the glorious autumns which follow."

"You know what day this is?" Anselm retorted heartily. "You know what happened eight years ago?"

"My brother was killed" Henry answered. "He died in the New Forest, an arrow to his heart. I rode to Winchester like the very wind. I seized the treasury and later the Crown and – " he jabbed a finger in Anselm's direction, " – brought you home in accordance with the customs and laws of this country, not to mention those of Holy Mother Church."

"You're being blunt, Sire," Anselm retorted, "so let me be equally honest and direct back. I have invited you here because it is your brother's anniversary eight years on. This morning I celebrated a Mass for the repose of his soul." He ignored Robert of Meulan's sardonic laugh.

"What is it?" Henry now had the bit between his teeth like a destrier, a warhorse, eager to begin. "What is it, Father, about my brother's death which concerns you?"

"He was King!" Anselm replied.

"He was a tyrant," Robert of Meulan broke in. "A King who exiled you, seized the treasure of the Holy Mother Church and plundered it to his heart's content."

"And you served him," Anselm replied, "as did your brother."

"But, Reverend Father," Queen Mathilda's voice was melodious, soft and honey-sweet, "Father, why now, why do you wish to see us about it?"

"Because those things," Anselm sighed, "which are in the dark are best brought into the light my Lady, including your part in these matters."

Mathilda stiffened.

"Reverend Father, what do you mean?"

"My Lord – " Anselm turned to the King, " – you and the Queen, you knew each other well before your brother died."

The King shrugged.

"Yes or no?" Anselm insisted.

"Of course we did."

"So you kept it well hidden?"

Henry laughed. "That was logical, that was necessary but as the Queen has asked, why now?"

Anselm got to his feet flicking crumbs from his gown. "I have – " he gestured at me, " – made the most careful study of all accounts of King William's death – be it written or verbal …"

"Gossip, tittle-tattle," Meulan scoffed.

"One piece perhaps," Anselm retorted, "but not all. We monks are scribes and listeners. Our Chroniclers spread their nets and catch all manner of things, even the truth. In the courts, a judge will be presented with a 'billa' – a case to answer." He walked across and stood over Meulan. "So don't be anxious my Lord, there must be a logical answer to all this! I certainly look forward to hearing it. Tonight," Anselm added, "you will be my guests at my supper. We shall talk about these matters then."

The rest of the day was taken up with preparations for the great evening feast. I glimpsed the King and his Queen, together with his councillors, sitting in the rose garden heads together, probably discussing the real reason why Anselm had invited them to St Augustine's. I went to the kitchens and made sure that my master's orders had been carried out. In truth the cooks surpassed themselves, preparing baked lamprey, fresh loaches with roses and almonds, pork puddings, cutlets of venison, grilled pike, spiced pancakes, followed by elderberry funnel cakes, whilst the abbey vinter had drawn up from the cellar small casks of the best Bordeaux and some white wine, kept in the frigidarium, especially imported from the Rhinelands.

We met early in the evening in the Prior's private parlour, a tastefully decorated chamber with sculptured ceiling, coloured cloths against the walls, fresh reeds soaked in herbs and specially dried, strewn across the floor. A great table ran down the centre of the parlour. At both ends stood throne-like chairs for the King and Queen with others ranged along each side. The shutters of the windows were open, allowing in the fragrance from the nearby garden. Small scented braziers were ready to be fired just in case the evening turned a little cold; clear evidence my master intended this banquet to be a long one. We all gathered there as the bells of the abbey church tolled for vespers. At first the conversation was general as servants came in and out with goblets of white wine and deliciously baked shortbread. At last Father Anselm indicated to the chamberlain who ushered the guests to their chairs; the meal was served, one course after another, the guests relaxing in the splendid occasion. The King openly complimented Anselm on his cooks, the tasty dishes, the splendid table with its white linen cloth and exquisite silver salt-cellar standing in the middle, the candelabra of gold and silver glittering with light. A sombre chamber transformed gloriously by the tapestries, candle-flame and the dying sunshine pouring through the windows. The wine jugs circulated while the conversation ebbed and flowed. For a while I discussed one of my master's works, *The Descent of the Holy Spirit*, with Duke Robert who seemed genuinely interested in questions of theology.

Eventually, at a sign from my master, the servants withdrew. Father Anselm himself got up to secure the door, looking into the passageway beyond before closing it firmly and doing the same with the window shutters.

"If it gets too hot," he smiled, "I can always open them again." He returned to where he sat between me and Count Robert of Meulan.

"Sire." He turned and bowed to the King then to the Queen sitting at the far end. Mathilda looked resplendent in a beautiful gold gown, her glorious hair now combed and falling in tresses down to her shoulders, a small veil on her head, a beautiful amethyst necklace round her swan-like throat.

"It is so good to see you all." Anselm leaned his elbows on the table and stared at the window. "It is," he murmured, "very good, and you must indulge me."

"Domine – " the King broke in respectfully, " – we are only too pleased to visit St Augustine's. Perhaps tomorrow we may go hunting with your permission?" This provoked chuckles and laughter amongst his companion. "But we are aware," the King continued, "that this is the eighth anniversary of my good brother's death. You wish to discuss that matter, Domine, why?"

"Why?" Anselm was still staring across the chamber. I could see he was preparing himself. "You must understand me, Sire, my Lords and you, my Lady." He smiled at Queen Mathilda. "But soon, I will have to present my final account to my Divine Master."

He quelled the protest by raising a hand. "There's work left to be done, but there again, that's the lot of any man, so many things I would like to do but cannot. My strength fails me. I grow weaker, ask Brother Eadmer here. However, one memory still haunts me, of William, King of the English, being struck by an arrow in the New Forest, dying without being shriven, without being hallowed or sanctified, his soul going straight to God."

"I have had Masses sung for him," Henry interposed, "many Masses. Surely the Lord in his great kindness …?"

"The Good Lord pardoned the repentant thief," Anselm agreed, "but I still have a debt. I have told you before, King and Archbishop, two oxen which, yoked together, pull the plough of this kingdom. I know my Lord – " he turned to Henry, " – we have fought, we have quarrelled, but those matters are now settled. I also quarrelled with your brother and that was never resolved, so I wish you to indulge me. I ask one great favour, let us examine the events surrounding his death."

"Why?" Robert, Count of Meulan broke in sharply, he slammed his goblet down on the table. "William the Red King is dead! Don't the Scriptures say leave the dead to bury the dead? As for his soul, that is a matter for God's mercy."

"Aye, my Lord," Anselm retorted, "and it's also a matter for God's justice."

"What do you mean?" Henry of Warwick spoke up, face flushed with wine. "What do you mean, Father, are you hinting at something wrong?"

"I am hinting at something mysterious."

Duke Robert who'd drunk fast and deep now seemed to sober. He was about to pick up his wine cup but he moved to grasp the beautifully sculptured glass carrying fresh water from the abbey well. He gulped this and refilled it. Fitzhaimo sat surly-eyed, the Beaumont impassive. The more I studied these powerful men, including the King and his Queen, the more my suspicion grew that this was a path they certainly did not wish to tread.

They'd thought the death of the Red King had been forgotten, barred, a matter of history, of dim memory, of no-one ever bothering, but my master was different.

"Let us seek the truth," Anselm began, as if posing a theological question in the schools.

"The truth!" Fitzhaimo almost bellowed ignoring the King's raised hand. "The truth, my Lord, is that William the Red King was accidentally killed by an arrow: the person responsible was Walter Tirel, but he fled. It was an accident! Some people claim the arrow was directed by God's vengeance, and God knows the late King had a great deal to answer for, including his treatment of you. It was an accident, what more is there to say?"

"Was it?" Anselm moved his head sideways to ease the tension at the back of his neck. "You were all there that day, I mean apart from my Lady and, of course, Ralph de Aquis."

I'd never heard that name before, its effect on the assembled company was certainly dramatic. The King's jaw dropped. Fitzhaimo coughed and straightened in his chair whilst Robert of Meulan glanced swiftly across the table at his brother.

"Ralph de Aquis," Anselm repeated, "the huntsman. He was certainly there at the hunting lodge at Brockenhurst and during the hunt, yet my Lords, I have searched for him the length and breadth of this kingdom but I still cannot find him."

"Ralph de Aquis?" Duke Robert slurred.

"A huntsman in the Royal household." Anselm replied. "He was present on 2nd August 1100 but he's now vanished. Most accounts describe Tirel as the Red King's slayer, others talk of a 'quidam miles' – 'a certain soldier' but one, without giving any reason, whispers 'Ralph de Aquis' – 'Ralph of Bath'." He turned, squeezed my wrist and winked. "I am sorry, Eadmer," he murmured, "but I was waiting to discover more – yet I have not!" He leaned closer. "And one other thing," he whispered, "but patience. Forgive me, Brother, you will soon know all."

I smiled and sketched a blessing. Anselm squeezed my wrist

again and looked round the table; he now had their full attention. "So," he continued, "Lammas Day, the first day of August, the beginning of the grease-season. William the Red King, his brother and leading nobles moved into the New Forest to hunt. They lodged at Brockenhurst. The King was in good heart, he had successfully defeated his enemies in France such as Helias of Maine, he had even threatened the territory of King Philip around Paris. Rumours were rife that the Duke of Aquitaine was to mortgage his Duchy to William. No threat had emerged at home, the treasury was full, the only slight fly in the ointment – " he laughed sharply and pointed a finger at Duke Robert, " – was you, my Lord, coming home from the Crusades, a knight, a Warrior of Christ, who'd borne the Cross and fought valiantly to defend the Holy Sepulchre."

Robert blushed slightly, pushing his chair back, shuffling his feet. Once again his hand went out to his wine cup but he thought again and it dropped away.

"I," Anselm continued, "was in exile in France, sheltering in the house of the Archbishop at Lyons with no prospect of return. So my Lords, Lammas Day, the year of our Lord 1100 came and went. Then what happened?"

"We were all there," King Henry replied, "in the hunting lodge at Brockenhurst. You know how it was. On Lammas Day evening my brother had returned exhausted but full of excitement after the hunt. We dined in the Hall, all seated around the table on the dais, Walter Tirel and others were there. My brother was in good humour. Some tumblers and acrobats entertained him. He drank deep then retired."

"The royal chamber," Fitzhaimo spoke up, "is above the Great Hall. The Red King retired for the night. All lanterns and candles were extinguished. Early in the morning I was roused by a cry. I went into the King's chamber. He was sitting up in bed, dressed in his tunic. He was fumbling with tinder, trying to light a candle on the table beside the bed. I remember him sitting there;

he didn't look so fierce then. I called his retainers: lanterns and candles were lit."

"And William?"

"As I said, he was sitting on the edge of the bed. He cried out to the Virgin Mary and asked for more lights to be brought. I asked him what was wrong? The King said he felt feverish; his sleep had been polluted by nightmares. He dreamed how a physician had been letting blood, he'd cut a vein and his blood spurted out like that of a fountain blotting out the heavens."

"Was he ill?" Anselm asked.

"He complained of pains in his stomach, his bowels were loose. The smell in the chamber was foul. It was a hot summer's night so I opened the shutters. The King refused to go back to sleep. He was frightened."

"Frightened?" Duke Robert banged the table. "The Red King was never frightened! Henry, do you remember that time when he and I chased you through France and you took refuge in the Monastery of Mont St Michel? Oh it must have been – " Duke Robert passed his goblet from one hand to the other, " – yes, it must be 17 years ago. Anyway," he continued blithely drunk, "William was in his tent when he saw some of the enemy riding by. He immediately mounted his own warhorse and charged them. In the fight which followed his destrier was wounded. The King – " Duke Robert drummed the table with excitement, " – was thrown off, but one foot became stuck in the stirrup. An enemy knight was about to cut him down with a sword but William cried out: 'Have a care, I'm the King of England!' The knight recognised his voice, raised him to his feet and gave him his own horse instead. God's speech – " Robert slurped from his cup, " – the King vaulted into the saddle and asked who was responsible for bringing him down? The knight replied, 'Sire, it was I, but I didn't know you were the King!' Do you know what William said?" Duke Robert stared round at the ring of hard faces. "'By the Face of Lucca, from now on Sir you will be my man, and in my service you will get a proper reward for your courage and spirit.'" The Duke laughed loudly banging the table until he realised where he was and what had been said, then he sobered up and jabbed a finger at Fitzhaimo. "My brother, the Red King, was no coward!"

"I didn't say he was, but on that morning he was frightened, terrified by his nightmares."

"But if that was the case, Fitzhaimo," Anselm intervened, "why did you frighten him further? I heard a story of how a monk from foreign parts arrived at the hunting lodge with his own dream. How he'd seen in a vision the Red King entering a church, seize the crucifix between his teeth and hungrily gnaw its arms and legs. For a while the figure on the crucifix endured this but then he kicked the King to the floor and the Red King's mouth bellowed forth smoke and fire. A fantastical tale – is it true?"

"There were many omens," Fitzhaimo grumbled, "portents, prophecies. I'm not God!" he jibed.

"In truth, you're not," Anselm replied, "but, according to the evidence I have studied, you brought such a story to the King."

"I can't remember." Fitzhaimo stared round the table, a look of desperation in his eyes as if seeking comfort and support.

"There were many prophecies and signs," Robert of Meulan spoke up, hand dropping away from his mouth.

"Yes, there were." Anselm leaned over, plucked an apple from the bowl and, picking up a knife, began to peel the skin. He glanced at me and tapped his goblet. I quickly rose, took the jugs of red and white wine and went round the table refilling the goblets. Nobody refused or asked where the servants were? My master had issued strict instructions, after a certain time no-one else was to enter that chamber. "Let me see." Anselm continued. "The Red King spent the rest of that day in the hall of the hunting lodge. He ate and drank well. Most of you were there. He spoke mainly to Walter Tirel, Lord of Poix?"

"He'd certainly recovered his good spirits," Henry of Warwick replied, "but he was reluctant to go hunting, perhaps because of his bad dreams, the hideous stories he'd heard."

"Is that true?" Anselm sliced the apple and popped a piece into his mouth. "But William Rufus was frightened of nobody. He publicly mocked dreams and portents. He was a man passionate about hunting, why would he waste a day trembling in that hall?"

Henry of Warwick just stared back.

"Do you know what I think?" Anselm swallowed what he was eating. "William the King was waiting for his stomach to settle, that's the truth isn't it? After all, later on that same day, another warning was delivered. A monk journeyed all the way from St Peter's in Gloucester. He'd been sent by Abbot Serlo to describe the vision of one of his monks. How he'd seen in a dream the Lord Jesus enthroned in heaven, being approached by the most beautiful, radiant-looking virgin who represented this Kingdom of England." He paused and pointed his knife at the Queen. "Of course that could have been an image of you sheltering in a nunnery in the south-west, pining for him – " Anselm gestured at Henry, " – wondering what would happen, when would your day of deliverance arrive?"

"I do not know." Mathilda flailed her hand. "I do not know …" Her voice trailed off.

"I have heard the same stories about warnings," Henry spoke up sharply, eager to divert the conversation. "But what have they really got to do with us? Are we here, my Lord Archbishop, to talk about dreams and visions which happened eight years ago and, if we are …" he scraped back his chair so as to break the tension, "those visions told the truth. My brother harassed the Church, plundered its riches, vexed its leaders, sent you into exile. I have done everything to restore harmony."

"What you have done," Anselm replied, "is what you are supposed to do, my Lord – God's will, but bear with me." He smiled. "Let us go back to the events of that day. You say the King dallied in the hall conversing with Walter Tirel." Anselm paused, no-one spoke. The Queen drank quickly, dabbing her mouth with a napkin, when she put the goblet down her hand trembled slightly.

"Why did the Red King delay?" Anselm placed the apple and knife down and spread his hands. "As I have said, he was waiting for his stomach to settle. He'd now eaten and drunk, and William did like his wine, but why did he go hunting so late? Why didn't he wait for the morrow, what was the haste?"

"He was a keen hunter," Henry snapped, "he didn't want to waste an entire day."

"But surely he was urged on?" Anselm asked. "You did encourage him – that's what I've read." There was no dissent. "And then there was the business of the arrows." Anselm picked up the knife, studying its tip. "I understand there is a tradition amongst hunters for the host to give a special guest a present, be it a bow, spear or arrows. Well, when King William was preparing for his hunt in the late afternoon, someone approached him. In one story it's a blacksmith, in another a huntsman. He presented the Red King with six specially made arrows. The King accepted these. He kept four for himself and, as is the custom, gave two to his closest friend and comrade who at the time was Walter Tirel, Lord of Poix. My Lord of Meulan, am I correct?"

Meulan was no longer sitting crookedly, but glaring at Anselm. Now Meulan is a warrior, he'd fought at Senlac and countless other battles, but sitting next to Anselm and catching his gaze, I glimpsed the fear in Meulan's eyes. My master himself was hunting but a different quarry from some hapless deer and he was drawing very close.

"Well?" Anselm asked. "Isn't that the truth? Tirel was the King's closest confidant and he received those arrows as a public mark of favour?"

"It is as you say," Meulan conceded. "The King gave two of the arrows to Tirel saying it was only fitting for the deadliest shot to get the sharpest arrows, or words to that effect."

"Good, good," Anselm murmured. "So we move on. The King was dressed for the hunt, the horses were brought into the yard, saddles thrown over, harnesses prepared. The King mounted: he left the hunting lodge moving south-east into the Forest."

"And there it ended," Henry intervened sharply. "Everyone," he jabbed a finger at the table, "everyone in this chamber accompanied me, whilst my brother and Tirel galloped off in another direction. There were other groups as well. It was early evening, still and calm. Noise travelled: the barking of dogs, the braying of horns, the neighing of horses and then it happened."

"What did?" Anselm asked.

"You know full well!" Meulan replied. "The King was hunting a deer, a stag roused by him. In the confusion Tirel loosed an arrow, it struck the King in the heart, he broke off the shaft and fell to the ground, apparently driving the point deeper into his chest. Panic ensued. Royal servants came looking for us. We were in a different part of the forest. By the time we reached the edge of the glade, the King was dead and Tirel had fled for his life. Other servants were milling about – consternation and confusion reigned. Men became very fearful, some just panicked and fled."

"And you, my Lord?" Anselm turned to the King. "You rode straight to Winchester and seized the treasury, proclaiming yourself King. You brushed aside the objections of others who believed that both treasure and crown belonged to Duke Robert, your brother."

"In truth, they belonged to no-one," Henry retorted, ignoring the drunken laugh from his brother. "Robert here was still returning from the Holy Land. There was no King. My brother had no heir. If I had not seized the crown and secured the treasury, civil war could have broken out, pillaging, plunder. I was, I am, of the royal blood," he added fiercely. "My right to the throne was as good as my father's or any of my brothers', I was there – the leading men of the country supported me."

"You could have waited!" Robert yelled.

"Why, brother, for you to arrive?" Henry taunted. "You, who take your time with everything? You, who couldn't hold Normandy, let alone England?"

"Peace, peace," Anselm soothed. He smiled across the table at Duke Robert. "Let us go back to that glade on that Thursday evening 2nd August, the year of Our Lord, 1100. Sire, my Lords, you arrive there. I can understand the shock, the confusion, but your King was dead. He was a man anointed and hallowed, who had sat on the throne of the Confessor and wore his Crown. He had received the chrism of holy anointing at the hands of the great Lanfranc. He now lay like a beggar man, forsaken in a forest glade, and you did nothing? Did you send for a priest so that he could be shriven?" Silence greeted Anselm's words. "Did you feel for any blood beat in his throat?" Again silence. "Ah well," Anselm sighed, "let's imagine that corpse lying on the edge of the glade. The day is drawing to a close, the sun is setting. To be sure, your haste and fear are understandable, you had to impose order. It is the King's function to protect his subjects, but let's leave that for the moment. How did you know that Tirel was the man responsible? Did someone see him shoot the King? Recently, I went to a nearby glade. I asked two of my lay-brothers, Oderic and Waltheof, who used to be bowmen, to accompany me into a small copse of trees. Targets were set up and they loosed arrows at them, even though I was watching exactly what they did, it was very difficult to say precisely which bowman loosed which arrow. In a hunt it is even more difficult, you are watching a quarry; very rarely does someone watch the hunter, the arrow being loosed, its flight and then whether it hits the mark or not. You watch one of these, not all. So who saw Tirel? Who watched him loose? Who studied the flight of his arrow? Who saw it hit the Red King?"

"They were alone," Fitzhaimo broke in.

"Precisely," Anselm agreed. "So, if they were alone who was the witness? Sire – " Anselm turned to the King, " – in the eight years since your brother died have you ever made any enquiry into the truth about what happened there?"

"Why should I?" Henry retorted. "William was the third member of our blood line to be killed in the forest. It was an accident."

"But who was the witness to this accident?" Anselm persisted.

"We could tell by the arrow," Henry of Warwick replied.

"Of course, of course," Anselm murmured, "those famous arrows, the ones the Red King had so publicly given to Tirel. You could tell couldn't you, from the shaft, the flight feathers?"

Henry of Warwick looked away, Meulan just shrugged.

"And Tirel himself," Anselm persisted, "why didn't anyone pursue him – if it was an accident, I mean?" Anselm cut a piece of apple and chewed it slowly. "Tirel was a stranger here. How could a man guilty of regicide, ride through a forest at night-time, reach Pevensey, board a ship and escaped unscathed? I know, I know." Anselm raised a hand, "You're going to talk about the confusion, that it was an accident, that Tirel must have fled through the darkness before news of the King's death became public. How Tirel used his status, power and wealth to board a ship and secure passage, but you have never asked him to return have you?"

"He is free to come and go as he wishes," Henry declared. "I have not seized his holdings in Essex."

"But you have never asked him to return?" Anselm repeated. "Ah well, I have." He smiled at the consternation his words caused. "Of course I have. You must know I would. Walter Tirel, Lord of Poix, is a friend of mine. I met him when I was a monk at Bec. His family were friends and patrons of the monastery where I studied. I have entertained him. Do you know – " Anselm moved in his chair, " – he may even have been brought to England by King William as a possible mediator with me when I was in exile."

Anselm pushed back his chair and produced a set of keys from the pocket of his gown. He rose and walked across to the side table and the small iron-bound coffer which stood between the silver gilt-edged cross and the bronze aquamanile carved in the shape of a charging knight. Anselm inserted the keys, opened the coffer and took out a small scroll. The parchment was fresh and white, the green ribbon round it recently cut. Anselm undid the small scroll, brought it back to the table and, stretching across, pulled a candlestick closer.

"I asked Walter Tirel to join us tonight, but of course he declined. He refuses to discuss this issue. He didn't write much, just a few words, so listen to this, my Lords. No – " he put his hand up, " – I will not tell you what precisely he says. However, Tirel has taken the most solemn of oaths, without fear or favour, that on day the Red King was killed, he neither went to that part of the wood where the King hunted or even caught sight of him in the wood. He invokes God's judgement on his soul that he is innocent of the deed." Anselm rolled the piece of scroll up and pushed it up the sleeve of his gown. "Walter Tirel is a man of honour." he continued. "He has sworn by his own immortal soul that he was nowhere near the Red King on that fateful evening. I believe him. He didn't write that it was an accident, for which he has purged himself and done reparation; he denies it completely. So, if Walter Tirel didn't loose that arrow, then who did?"

"If he's innocent," Meulan countered, "then why does he not come back here, why doesn't he tell us more?"

"True," Anselm mused. "I've reflected on the same – " He patted his sleeve, " – but that's all Tirel will say – has said. I wonder why?"

"And?" Fitzhaimo asked.

"Tirel won't return because he is a very frightened man – and, again, I wonder why?"

There was a long moment of stillness. I remember it well. From the nearby church echoed the lucid song of a chorister singing the famous carol 'Vir ait falsus' – 'The liar said':

I was to
Heaven translated.
I saw Christ there
Sitting and
Joyfully
Feasting.
John, called the
Baptist, was
Cupbearer,
Handing round
Goblets of
Excellent
Wine to the
Saints.
The Bishop
Remarked: 'Wisely
Did Christ choose
The Baptist
To be his
Cupbearer,
Because he
Is known not
To drink any
Wine.
But you are
A liar to
Say that St
Peter is
Head of the
Cooks, when he
Guards Heaven's
Gate.

The words, with their mocking allusion to truth and lies, charged the atmosphere of that banqueting chamber. The wine, the good meats, the soft bread and the ripe fruit were all forgotten. It was as if the room had subtly changed – no longer a prior's parlour with its carved beam ceiling, rich cloths and drapes decorating the walls, comfortable furnishings and precious objects glittering in the candle and lamp light. The air no longer smelt sweetly of beeswax and the flavours of fine food. It was as if an angel from heaven had descended to move the assembled company back in time to that lonely glade, in that haunted forest so many years ago, a morning when Rufus had been roused from his sleep to face his own death and so begin the last day of his life, which ended not in an accident, but murder. I stared at all their faces, Meulan, that cunning serpent, that veritable fox of a man slumped in his chair, one hand masking the lower half of his face. He was staring across at his brother. I wondered what that stare meant. Fitzhaimo, red hair all spiked, sat as if carved out of stone, only a muscle high in his cheek twitched and jerked, a sign of his inner fury, or fear. Henry the King clutched his goblet to his chest. At the far end of the table Mathilda the Queen straightened up, bracing her shoulders as if trying to relieve some discomfort and pain, her blue eyes were agate-hard and staring, her lower lip quivering as if on the verge of tears. Only Duke Robert stayed relaxed. He lounged, a stupid smile on his silly face as if savouring some secret joke. My master seemed younger. Anselm's face had grown smoother, a colouring to the flesh, a sparkle to the eye – like he used to be in the schools when he debated some theological point or the logic of some hypothesis. Only then did I truly realise how Anselm passionately believed that a hideous crime had been committed. William the Red King had been murdered. In the Old Testament, after Cain had killed his brother, God had pursued Cain across the face of the earth, seized him and marked him as an assassin. Anselm was about to do the same. One of these people sitting at table with him was a Judas, a betrayer, a killer. Anselm, the lamb, had trapped the wolves. If he wanted to be, Anselm could be the holy man, the austere Benedictine; true, he was a poor monk but he was also Archbishop of Canterbury, Head of the Church in England, 'Legatus a latere Papae – Papal Legate', the representative of Christ's Vicar on earth. He had the full power of excommunication, to curse with bell, book and candle and so damn a Christian soul to the roaring fires of eternal hell.

The moment of stillness and silence continued. The King's ministers and his wife stared at their royal master. If he gave the signal they would rise and abruptly leave, but that would be an admission of guilt. Anselm would pursue them like the Furies. He had shown them the road he intended to go down and they would have no choice but to follow. Henry gave a great sigh and sat back in his chair staring up at the ceiling beams, fingers beating a rhythm on the arm of the chair. He sighed again and raised his hand slightly, a sign to the rest that they must stay.

"Tirel is lying!" Meulan barked, half-rising from his chair. Anselm gestured at him to sit.

"He is lying!" Meulan repeated. "He loosed the arrow! He killed the King, then he fled."

"I don't think so," Anselm retorted. "He had nothing to lose, nothing to gain by the death of the Red King. Now let us listen to his words carefully. Here is a man who has taken the solemnest oaths on his own eternal salvation. He doesn't say he was near the King, he actually says he was nowhere near the King that day. He never saw the King, which logically means he never saw the King either alive or dead. Accordingly, we must put his flight into a new context. The hunting party leave Brockenhurst and ride off. Tirel goes to another part of the forest. The killing takes place. Verderers and foresters are running about taking messages here and there. Tirel didn't see the King alive or dead," Anselm repeated, "so someone must have told him that he was now being held responsible. This must have occurred very shortly after the King had been struck." Anselm paused to collect his thoughts. "So the Red King lies prostrate, an arrow to his chest, Tirel is in another part of the forest. Somebody must have gone looking for Tirel. Someone in authority whom Tirel would trust, telling him that the King was dead. Someone also who could recognise the arrow as one of those given to Tirel by William, so that person must have been very close to the King in the hall of the hunting lodge earlier that day. Strange," Anselm mused, "according to some Chronicle accounts, Tirel was actively helped out of the Kingdom. Did this person, whoever it was, assure Tirel that an arrow from his bow had killed the King then advise and help Tirel to reach the port of Pevensey? In which case there are two logical conclusions. First, the man who warned Tirel acted very swiftly. There was no dilly-dallying around the King's body, this person went immediately looking for Tirel."

"And secondly?" Henry asked.

"Tirel himself must have realised the terrible danger he was in. If he was in a different part of the forest, if he hadn't even seen the King, let alone loosed that arrow, then he realised that he was being cast as the scapegoat. He'd be terrified. He realised that there was no other choice but to flee England, return to France and never come back."

"Are you accusing us?" Henry demanded beating his fist on the table. "My Lord Archbishop, are you accusing me of murder?"

"I am accusing someone," Anselm retorted, "but, my Lord, bear with me. Let us reach the logical conclusion. Let us return to that glade. Walter Tirel had been advised that one of his arrows had struck the King and that he should flee. Who would do that – anyone here?" A chorus of denials greeted these words. "But somebody must have, someone quick-witted who knew what was going to happen. I've scrutinised the old household rolls," Anselm continued, "I've come up against one man's name, Ralph de Aquis – Ralph of Bath, a huntsman. I have searched for him everywhere. I have sent messengers out. Now he seems to have disappeared yet he was definitely at the hunting lodge at Brockenhurst on that fateful day. I also believe, as a principal huntsman, Ralph gave the King those arrows, two of which were given to Tirel. I believe Ralph de Aquis was nearest to the King when he was struck by that arrow, and immediately went off to warn Tirel."

"Are you saying that this Ralph is the assassin?" Meulan asked.

"Oh yes," Anselm replied. "Many accounts talk of the King being alone except for one companion. I can imagine how it happened. Ralph de Aquis, the huntsman, the organiser, the paid assassin – " Anselm emphasised the last words, " – would organise the hunt surely? He sent you off didn't he? Different groups in different places, that was why Tirel was nowhere near the Red King. He was the last person Ralph de Aquis wanted to be present when the murder took place – the King's close friend and confidant? No, de Aquis arranged it so that only he and the Red King were alone in that glade. He also made sure, and he'd be responsible for such weapons, that the royal bow Rufus was carrying was faulty, its cord snapped. I wondered about the significance of that, it was the only useful weapon the King carried. Let us say, for sake of argument, that Ralph de Aquis was the assassin: he would loose the shaft at the King, but the King may well have moved, the arrow might have missed its mark. The King may have realised he was in great danger, the one weapon he had for defence was his bow, but its string was already snapped, it was useless to him. The King was vulnerable to a second arrow if one was needed. One other thing I cannot understand, my Lords, is a matter I have already raised." Anselm lifted his goblet and sipped carefully. "The King is dead, or so they say, struck to the heart by an arrow, but no attempt was made to fetch a priest for him to be shriven. More importantly, my Lords, did you ever truly discover whether the King was dead or not?"

"An arrow to the heart," Fitzhaimo scoffed, "of course he was dead!"

"No, he wasn't," Anselm replied. "The King was still bleeding, blood gushing from the wound, when he was put onto Purkell's cart and taken back to Winchester. He was dying, but not dead. Do you realise that? The King of England, slowly dying, bleeding to death like a stuck pig, whilst you dart ahead to seize the crown and treasury. By the time the royal cortège reached Winchester the following morning, William would be truly dead due to severe loss of blood. What happened then, my Lords? Was the corpse bathed, anointed, laid in State? I don't think so." Anselm shook his head. "By that evening, you were galloping to London to arrange your coronation."

"The corpse was handed over to the good brothers at Winchester," Henry of Warwick blustered. "Matters were pressing, the body was buried quickly. Domine …" Henry of Warwick, known for his diplomacy, had sat listening intently to what Anselm had been saying. "Whether the King died instantly or not, he would never have survived. We cannot act the hypocrites and mourn. The Red King was a sinner, a prince who publicly boasted that he did not fear God nor man, who plundered the Church. Surely people could not be expected to weep tears, to put on pomp and ceremony in what would really be an empty show? He was buried. We had other pressing matters to deal with."

"I have had prayers and masses offered for his soul," Henry shouted. "Good silver for priests to sing the Requiem."

"I am sure you have," Anselm declared, "but, my Lord King, you had no love for your brother, did you?"

Henry chewed the corner of his lip.

"And William did not trust you," Anselm continued remorselessly. "Tell me, Sire, at the beginning of the King's reign, you rebelled against William didn't you? He later besieged you at Mont St. Michel where you had to surrender. He taught you a lesson you never forgot. One you acted on. Never show your true face publicly, never reveal your emotions, never speak honestly. It must have been a great insult for you to be brought to heel by William the Red King, given a warning never to do it again."

"He certainly didn't like you," Duke Robert scoffed. "Do you remember when we had you bolted up like a rabbit in its warren at Mont St Michel?"

"Shut up!" Henry bawled.

The Death of the Red King

"Why should I?" Duke Robert replied hotly. "I saved you then! You were all locked up and running short of water. You sent a messenger to William about why should you be deprived of something which was provided for all men to enjoy? I, not William, sent you the water. I remember the Red King laughing! A fine sort of general, he accused me, sending water to the enemy! How could we possibly defeat him if I provided him with food and drink? Do you know my reply, brother?" Robert hit the table. Beneath his bonhomie a real rage seethed in the Duke's heart. "'Do you really think'," Robert continued, "this is what I said to William, 'that we should condemn our own brother to death by thirst? What other kin would we have if we lost you?'" He paused, fighting for breath. "Did you kill William?" he taunted.

Anselm quickly intervened lest the quarrel grew more violent.

"You, Sire, certainly had no love for the Red King" Anselm repeated. "He never trusted you. On many occasions he left England to go to Normandy for war, or some other business, but never once were you given any position of high office, never left as *Custos Regni* – Keeper of the Realm, Regent? It must have been demeaning to see William the King put more trust in the likes of Flambard than his own brother. William kept an eagle eye on you. He watched your every move. Oh, you owned land in England but nothing significant, this office or that sinecure, but nothing important. You were constantly in the King's company, because that's where he wanted you to be so he could watch you. He allowed Flambard to plunder your possessions, didn't he? There were other matters. Do you remember Anskill? A knight who held land off the Abbot of Abingdon? False allegations were levelled against him. King William imprisoned him and starved him to death. Anskill left a widow, Ansfrida, as well as a son. The Red King showed little pity for them. He seized the Manor of Sparsholt from her and gave it to someone else. Ansfrida came to you, my Lord King, to beg for your intercession. She later became your mistress." Anselm ignored the Queen's sharp hissing sigh. "She bore you a son. You went and pleaded with the Red King, but he refused your petition. You must have hated him for that!"

"I did not like my brother," Henry replied. "His ways were his and mine were mine, but are you claiming I killed him? I was in a different part of the forest that day. Moreover, my Lord Archbishop, I am surrounded here by great Lords who had faithfully supported my brother, why should they allow me, as you say, without lands, without honours, without titles, to kill the King, their patron? You have no evidence I acted treacherously against him."

"But I do," Anselm interrupted. "The proof is in this very room." Anselm pointed down the table at the Queen sitting like some marble statue, all colour drained from that beautiful face. Her lips seemed bloodless, her eyes larger and darker. She was staring at Henry as if she'd been confronted by something which she herself had nursed in the deepest recesses of her soul.

"What do you mean?" Henry declared.

"Your brother died in August. Within three months you had married Mathilda and had her crowned as Queen."

"You were always opposed to that marriage," the King declared.

"I have told you," Mathilda's voice was now not so soft and loving but strident and carrying. "I have told my Lord Archbishop I was no nun!"

"Of course you were not," Anselm replied. "But you did love each other. You had met long before your marriage took place. To do that would need great subterfuge. After all, my Lady, you were in cloisters. You had, according to some people, taken the veil, you were a nun consecrated to God, above all you are the descendant of Saxon Kings, royal blood flows in your veins. Did Henry see you as a prize? A joyous union between the Houses of the Conqueror and Godwinson? Of Normandy and England? You both must have met secretly, so, my Lord, you and your wife were already conspiring against the Red King. If you can plot on one matter, why not another?" Anselm laid his fingers flat on the table. "And then, of course, it happened. Duke Robert of Normandy was coming home." Anselm pointed at Robert. "You, my Lord, were the catalyst; the all conquering Christian hero, the great Crusader! Can you imagine the effect of your return on a kingdom where your brother was cursed by every churchman, be it monk, priest, chaplain, abbot, bishop and archbishop? And of course there was me." Anselm shrugged. "The direct cause of the Red King's death. I, the Archbishop of Canterbury, had been driven into exile, my lands seized, my treasures ransacked, other churches throughout the kingdom had been plundered. William had overstretched himself. In my letters to the Holy Father I explained how I could not excommunicate the Red King because, in such circumstances, I would be both plaintiff and judge and that is against natural justice. However, the situation in this kingdom could not continue. Here was a King acting as if he was Pope, as if he owned Church lands and offices. Sooner or later, and I suspect sooner rather than later, Pope Paschal would have intervened and what then? He would excommunicate the Red King. The Pope would declare him deposed. He would say that every man's hands should be against him. William Rufus would be cursed with bell, book and candle, condemned to hell whilst anyone who took up arms against him would be doing God's work – in other words a new Crusade. Can you imagine how the Red King's enemies abroad would have loved that? Philip of France, Helias La Flèche, David of Scotland, and of course, any discontented great lord in England or Normandy would rally to the sacred banner of the great crusader, Duke Robert." Anselm paused. "In this kingdom it has happened before."

"Our own father!" Duke Robert exclaimed.

"Precisely," Anselm agreed. "When the Conqueror took up arms against Harold Godwinson, he appealed to Hildebrand, Pope Gregory VII, to approve his cause, alleging Harold was a usurper.

Pope Gregory agreed. He sent your father a papal banner, divine confirmation through Christ's Vicar on earth, of the justness of his quarrel with Godwinson. Pope Paschal might well have done the same."

"But it did not happen," Meulan intervened. "That did not happen and I doubt if it ever would."

"Nonsense," Anselm retorted. "Shortly after the Red King was killed, a papal legate arrived in this country. He came to warn the Red King but, of course, his abrupt death in the New Forest, as well as the policies, you Sire, had adopted, published and proclaimed, removed any need for him to act. No, no, if the Red King had not been killed, you, Duke Robert, would have become the champion, the holder of the papal banner, the divinely appointed vengeance against an infidel King. So let me ask – " Anselm leaned his elbows on the table, " – what would you have done then, Henry of England? Where would you have stood? What a hideous dilemma for you and the other great lords? If you stayed with William you would have also been God's enemies, excommunicated, damned for all eternity to hell fire. If William your brother went down, he would drag you with him. However, if you separated yourself from your brother, you might well be on God's side but, that does not necessarily mean that of the victors. If that happened, what then? You, my Lord King, many years ago had already rebelled against your kingly brother and been taught a sharp lesson. What would happen next time? Moreover, I have described Duke Robert's celebrated return but did you really have confidence in his military ability? Let us forget about papal curses, the visions and dreams of monks. What would actually have happened on the battlefield? If the Red King was victorious what would be the fate of a younger brother like yourself, a rebel who'd taken part in a revolt and been defeated? You would have been driven out of England, out of Normandy, with no lands, no revenues and certainly no chance – " Anselm waved to the Queen sitting like a snow-maiden at the end of the table, " – no love, no wife. You would have become a wanderer, an exile in foreign courts, eating black bread, accepting charity, no place to call your own. Moreover, time was passing, you were over 30 years of age when your brother was killed, Mathilda was 20, there was an urgency both to your love as well as your need to act."

Anselm stopped speaking. The atmosphere in the chamber was like that of a court-hall when the sentence of death was about to be announced and the executioner readies his noose. Anselm blithely ignored this but, picking up a taper, began to light more of the candles and then refilled everyone's goblet. The King, his great lords and his lovely Queen sat expectantly. I could almost guess what Henry's cunning brain was plotting; turning and twisting like a swallow beneath God's heaven. What did Anselm truly intend? Was he there as judge and executioner, or something else? Anselm blew the taper out, sat down in the chair and lifted his own goblet. He toasted the assembled company and, turning, whispered to me. "Eadmer, remember this." He squeezed my wrist gently and gestured with his goblet at Fitzhaimo.

"What would happen to you, my Lord, fighting to control your lands in the south-west and along the Welsh Marches. You exercise a lot of influence there, don't you? You're a great patron of the Abbey of St Peter of Gloucester and its daughter house at Tewkesbury: the same place, the same area where you, my Lady, were in a convent at Wilton, the same region which gave rise to so many of those visions and dreams of monks prophesying the Red King's death. Were such portents subtly prompted by you Fitzhaimo? Did you sow the seeds, hint and whisper that something was about to happen? You, especially – " Anselm pointed at Fitzhaimo, " – had a great deal to lose in any war between Duke Robert and the Red King. You have many opponents in the south-west and along the Welsh border. Nobles like Robert de Belleme. If you'd lost, all you had would become theirs. Whilst you – "

"You'd have nothing!" Robert bawled drunkenly. "You would have got nothing from me!"

"Yes, you would have got nothing," Anselm agreed, "and you, my Lord of Meulan, what could you expect from a duke who had once imprisoned you, seized your property and given it to another? Indeed, what would have happened to all your Norman possessions when Duke Robert, allied to Philip of France and Helias La Flèche – supported by the Pope as well as by every priest and monk in Normandy and England – swept to war, in defence – " Anselm mockingly beat his breast, " – of poor Archbishop Anselm, so cruelly driven into exile by the perfidious Red King?" Anselm smiled at Duke Robert. "Surely this is the song you would have sung."

The Duke smiled drunkenly back. "Oh yes," he slurred, "I knew the tune and all its verses. A sweet song," he openly mused, cradling his goblet. "I was the Expected One." He put down the goblet and flung out his arms. "The Messiah, the Avenger waiting at the door with his winnowing fan to sort the wheat from the chaff. Much good," he snorted, "it did me!"

"But at the time," Anselm insisted, "the harvest was ripe for cutting. Duke Robert was approaching the borders of Normandy, the possible father of a future prince. More importantly he was armed with his wife's dowry to pay the mortgage on his duchy as well as hire mercenaries and recruit men. So – " Anselm rose from his chair and walked to stand behind that of the King, " – what would happen to you?" Anselm slowly walked down the length of the table and stood by the Queen's chair. "Even if Duke Robert hadn't returned, what if the Red King had found out about your secret passion for Mathilda, a direct descendant of the Royal Saxon House? Would he force her to become a nun? Did he already suspect something was wrong? Was he going to marry her off to someone else like William de Warrene, Earl of Surrey? Is that why the Earl hated you so much my Lord King, and joined Duke Robert here? What could you all do?" Anselm walked back to his chair. "You may have loved the Red King, but he would not be advised, so when did you start plotting? You – " he pointed at Meulan, " – were already associated with Henry. I mean no offence but isn't it true – " he quickly bowed to the King, " – that Isabel de Meulan, my good lord's daughter, was your mistress, that she's even borne you a bastard child? You had so much in common and so much to lose. You wanted to keep your power. You were frightened the Red King might lose all in his stupid gamble. He refused to treat with me. He defied the Pope and openly mocked him. You all knew that situation could not last."

"You have planned this well, haven't you?" Meulan retorted. He half rose from his chair still clutching the knife which he'd used to cut his meat.

"Pax et bonum," Anselm whispered. "This is an Abbey, sacred ground. To even threaten me warrants excommunication!"

"Sit down, Meulan!" The King shouted. The Count did so.

"You have planned this well," Meulan whispered hoarsely, leaning across the table. "You invited us here as your friends only to confront us with this."

"I'm not your friend," Anselm replied. "Not for this evening, not for this short period of God-given time, but your judge. I suspect you, Meulan, were one of the principal movers in this. And you – " he gestured at Henry, " – did not need much encouragement." Anselm leaned across the table. "More importantly, I suspect that you, my Lord Meulan, were jealous of Walter Tirel, Lord of Poix. He had become the Red King's close friend and confidant, a man who accompanied him everywhere. However, Tirel was a stranger to this kingdom and was unable to warn the Red King. By the summer of 1100 the Red King was certainly in great danger and totally unaware of it, but you were. He could be swept away and you with him so you all started to plot. Somewhere, sometime you reached a decision: William Rufus had to die. It was easy to start the whispering campaign; the Red King's persecution of the church was now infamous. Fitzhaimo, with his power in the south-west, which included the convent where Mathilda sheltered, was well placed to fan the flames of rumour. It was easy enough, particularly as the monks of St Peter of Gloucester had recently witnessed the lechery and lasciviousness of the Red King's Christmas court and his way of living. Little wonder stories began to seep out about God's bow being stretched back, of the arrow being notched, of vengeance coming. You knew William would regard these as he always did – as mere smoke in the breeze. You were also aware that, come the greasetime, the Red King would adjourn to the New Forest to indulge his passion for hunting. The plot was set, the snare prepared."

"I wasn't party to it," Duke Robert protested.

"Oh yes, you were," Anselm replied. "Like me, whether you like it or not, you were swept up in events. You came home, Duke Robert. Sooner or later, if I'd stayed in exile, our paths would have crossed. You'd be the rallying point, I would be the cause. Anyway, on the evening of 1st August, whilst he was at Brokenhurst, either the King's meat or drink, or possibly both, were tainted. He suffered physical pain, anguish of the mind, he would be unable and, perhaps unwilling, to go hunting: that was important, the killing had to take place at night. News of the King's death would not spread so fast and perhaps not be published until the following morning. By then you, my Lord King, and your councillors would have seized both crown and treasury." Anselm paused to sip at his wine. "You had chosen both time and place well. The Red King could die hunting like the animal he was, in a forest many regarded as deeply cursed for the Great Conqueror's family – God's just judgement against the strict forest laws. After all, the Conqueror's other son, Richard, had been killed in the New Forest – "

"As had my bastard child ..." Duke Robert interrupted hastily.

"True," Anselm agreed. "Two accidents which demonstrated God's judgement, so why not let there be a third for the

The Death of the Red King

blasphemous Red King? Brockenhurst and Througham were ideal locations, close to the coast for Tirel, whilst Winchester was only a swift ride away, and from there, along the Roman road to London." Anselm paused. "The plot was set. Ralph de Aquis, that mysterious huntsman, appeared in the King's hall and drew close. In view of all he offered six arrows, William the Red King took four and gave two to Tirel. I am not too sure as I cannot prove if one of you here suggested that! On the grounds of logic I think you did. The Red King would only be too pleased to flatter Tirel. Now, it was only matter of waiting.

Later on that day you, Fitzhaimo and the rest encouraged the Red King to go hunting – not that William would need much encouragement. He'd risen from his bed sick and ill but now he'd recovered. He had eaten and drunk well, he didn't want to waste any more time, so he left. The only weapon he carried was his bow which had already been tampered with. Once you'd left the hunting lodge you all rode off to different parts of the forest and awaited events. The Red King, alone with Ralph de Aquis, was killed by an arrow similar to ones given to Tirel – " Anselm stared round, " – four for the King, two for Tirel. Who carried the seventh, the one which killed him? Ralph de Aquis, of course, that mysterious bowman whom no-one can now find? Who seems to have disappeared from the face of God's earth?" Anselm paused at the tolling of a bell deep in the Abbey. "God have mercy on Rufus' soul," he whispered. "This is his anniversary, the very hour, the very day. In God's eyes is there such a thing as time? Will the prayers I offer today for his soul be placed before God even as the Red King died? Ah well. On that night Walter Tirel was in a different part of the forest but he was warned about what had happened. He was allowed to flee. He had no choice. How could he stay to protest? He might face danger from some of the Red King's immediate retinue. Whatever the truth, who would believe him? Accident or murder, Tirel stood to lose both life and limb so he fled, the best thing for him, and for you. Once that happened you were all safe. You gathered round the Red King's corpse not caring whether he was alive or dead. The important thing was Winchester, the treasury, the crown. You, my Lord Henry, seized those, then you did two things which are most important. First, you issue a charter promising reform, a list of concessions and liberties. Secondly, you invite me back. You want me in England before Duke Robert arrives, before I'm seized by other people, before I'm persuaded perhaps not to return. You do remember that letter you wrote, possibly on the same day you were crowned? Not only were you desirous of me returning – " Anselm dug into his pocket and took out a copy of the letter, " – but you even told me which route to take. You write: 'I would have sent you some money by some of our courtiers but the death of my brother has caused such commotion throughout the dominion of England that they could by no means have reached you in safety.'" Anselm glanced up. "You see, my Lord, you knew what was about to happen: 'I therefore'," my master continued reading, 'advise you not to travel by Normandy but by Wissant and I will have my barons at Dover to meet you with money so that you will find, by God's help, the means to repay what you borrowed'. You conclude: 'Make haste then, Father, to come here so our Mother the Church of Canterbury, long agitated and distressed on your account, will no longer sustain any further loss of souls.' Very persuasive." Anselm rolled the scroll up. "You needed me in England for four reasons. You needed me to confirm your coronation, your seizure of the treasury and, above all, you wanted me out of harm's way. You certainly did not want me in Normandy. Strange isn't it?" Anselm mused. "Royal messengers can't reach me in Normandy because they might be stopped. Walter Tirel, Lord of Poix, however had no such difficulty in fleeing abroad."

"And the fourth reason?" Meulan broke in harshly.

"Oh, the fourth reason," Anselm bowed towards the Queen, "Mathilda. I was needed in England because you, Sire, fully intended to wed Mathilda and crown her Queen. The only person who could confirm that was me. You knew my doubts about whether she was free to marry or not, my agreement to it would clear the way of future difficulties."

"But you have no real proof for what you say," Henry of Warwick declared. "This is all supposition."

"I told my good friend Eadmer here – " Anselm patted me on the arm " – that this would not be solved by evidence but by logic. All those factors coming together: the portents; the omens; Duke Robert's return; Mathilda's marriage; my exile: growing papal opposition; the Red King's delay in hunting; the arrows; the haste to Winchester; Tirel's declaration; his good fortune to escape unscathed. True, I have not produced Ralph de Aquis but I challenge you, my Lord King, if I cannot find him, can you?"

Henry simply picked up his goblet and drank noisily.

"There is," Anselm spoke slowly, "one final hypothesis and stating it, I admit my own guilt." He took a deep breath. "At the end of 1099 I wrote a full and frank letter to Pope Paschal II: I accused the Red King of seizing the entire Church and driving me into exile. I virtually invited the Holy Father to excommunicate the English King. I believe that letter was copied and circulated. It certainly fed the feverish fires of prophecy and doom." He gestured round. "You must have seen it because your letter to me, Sire, at least in theory, resolved all my grievances. In retrospect that was insulting but I'm not here to answer insult but to concede that my letter, when you read it, forced you to act. However – " Anselm sipped from his wine cup " – I offer another hypothesis but it leads to the same conclusion. Naming Tirel as the Red King's slayer was a subtle deceit, especially as Tirel was known to me. Indeed he had been entertained by me. Would people also see God's will in that? The blasphemous Red King brought low, albeit accidentally, by a friend of the Great Victim, Anselm the exiled Archbishop? And if it was murder, well who knows, was the great Anselm involved?" My master raised his hand. "I fiercely resent that, yet it leads me to another hypothesis: William the Red King was no fool. He, too, must have seen the signs when he read my letter. At Brockenhurst, and the accounts declare this, he discussed serious business. Was the Red King going to make peace with me? Was Tirel to be his envoy, his intermediary? Is that what William, after he'd heard Abbot Serlo's warning, referred to when he asked Tirel to do justice in that matter? If a peace had been arranged between the Red King and myself, it would have resolved his problems, my problems – but certainly not yours, my Lord Henry? Once that accidental slaying took place, however," Anselm shrugged, "the Red King was no more, Tirel was discredited, in the eyes of many he still is." Anselm glanced around "What say ye?"

The King and his company stared stonily back.

"I am finished here," Anselm declared wearily, "I cannot say any more." He rose from the table, opened the shutters and stared out of the window, humming quietly beneath his breath.

"What next, my Lord Archbishop?" Meulan asked.

"What next?" Anselm turned. "I suppose it's futile to demand that Ralph de Aquis be searched for, taken up and questioned. I suspect that man's soul has already gone to God's tribunal to answer for whatever he did." Anselm went behind the King's chair. He leaned over and whispered in Henry's ear, so close as to be inaudible but the effect on Henry was dramatic. He visibly paled, eyes fearful. Anselm whispered again, then straightened up. "As for anything else – " my master walked to the door, beckoning me to follow him " – in the end, as I have said to the King, I will leave this to God. There's a saying isn't there, I've heard it many a time. How the mills of God grind exceedingly slow, but they do grind exceedingly small. In the final analysis – " he paused, his hand on the latch, " – a King was slain, his blood spilt – in itself a crime, a terrible sin, but to send his soul to God unprepared and unshriven! Didn't you ever think, my Lord King, at least to send for a priest to prepare your brother's soul for judgement? Anyway, my Lord King, Seigneurs, my Lady."

Anselm bowed. "You are my guests here. You may come and go as you please. I bid you goodnight."

Once outside the chamber he led me into the rose garden. It was deserted. Anselm sat me down on the bench next to him.

"Do you really think Henry will search for Ralph de Aquis?" I asked. "Was he the assassin?"

"There's one part of Tirel's letter I didn't quote. The accusation was too explicit," Anselm replied. "He said that the arrow may have been fired by the King himself."

"What do you mean?" I asked. "That is impossible. The Red King's bow was broken."

"No listen, Eadmer. Tirel was writing in the present day. He's terrified, rightly so. Perhaps it's the nearest he came to telling the truth: the arrow was loosed by the King himself but he is not referring to William."

"But to Henry!" I gasped. "That his own brother loosed the fatal arrow?"

"If Tirel is speaking the truth, Eadmer, and I think he is, then there were three men in that glade: William, Ralph de Aquis and Henry. Do you recall two of the accounts you studied? The first talked of the Red King shouting: 'Shoot, you devil. Shoot in the devil's name, shoot, or it will be the worse for you'. Strange remarks," Anselm mused. "Such dramatic and excitable language over a mere stag." Anselm chewed his lips. And that threat: 'shoot, you devil', and 'shoot, or it will be the worse for you'. Would William have used such language to a powerful magnate like Walter Tirel, Lord of Poix?"

"But Tirel wasn't there?"

"Exactly, Eadmer. Somebody else was – in fact two people: Ralph de Aquis and the person urging him on – "

"Henry, the King's brother?"

"In truth yes. His screaming at the assassin to loose – that account has become garbled and picked up by some monastic chronicler but it undoubtedly occurred."

"And the second source?"

"Again part of the propaganda. The story about Count Henry leaving the hunt and sheltering in a peasant's cottage because his bow string has snapped."

"Of course!" I exclaimed, "that hunt did not last long yet, strangest of coincidences …"

"Go on, Eadmer," Anselm urged.

"So, the Red King – no one knows where he was or who was with him but, on the other hand, Henry is placed precisely – he was not part of the hunt, having retired to a cottage."

"And?"

"Here are two royal brothers who went hunting late in the day yet, at the same time, in that same place, the Red King's bow string broke and so did his brother's."

"And the conclusion to all this?"

"The Red King's bow string was tampered with to leave him defenceless …"

"And Henry's?"

"To demonstrate that when his brother was killed, Henry was out of the hunt. His bow string had also snapped so he could not be held responsible."

"I agree." Anselm patted me on the shoulder. "Before we left I whispered to Henry the rest of Tirel's message, as well as what we have just discussed."

"Do you think Henry believes he has been indicted?"

"Perhaps," Anselm replied. He stared up at the night sky. "Only God knows what truly happened in that forest glade eight years ago but, Eadmer, at least I've discharged my duty. Rufus' soul has gone to God, I leave the rest in the hands of the good Lord."

"And what do you think Henry will do?" I asked.

Anselm pulled a face. "What he's done for the last eight years, Eadmer – nothing at all! Life will go on, a river of events, one day following another. But trust me, Brother – " he gestured back towards the refectory, " – one day the debt will have to be paid in full!"

VIII

Compline

For it is close, the day of their ruin.
Their doom comes at speed.
(Deuteronomy 32)

My master has crossed that gorge, the causeway crumbling behind him. He died at Easter the following year. He became too weak to stand, so had himself carried into chapel to hear Mass. He fell into unconsciousness on the eve of Palm Sunday. He gave his last benediction on Tuesday. On Wednesday morning after Matins, they laid him on the ash strewn floor and, by day break, his spirit had began its journey. He has survived the great challenge mounted against every soul. He has passed through the second death and emerged victorious. He is a Saint, a Lord at the Court of Light. My friend has gone. Now I am an old man, some 32 years after the events I have described here. I sit in my cell, bowed and rheumy-eyed. I know my time is coming, but I tell you, Anselm was right – evil begets evil. What we do not only echoes in Eternity but comes back shooting like an arrow. Fitzhaimo was dead within the year. Ten years later Mathilda died, loved by all, followed by Robert of Meulan of a broken heart due to the infidelities of his wife with Warenne, Earl of Surrey. Henry lived to reap the harvest. His only son, William, drowned when *La Blanche Nef*, the White Ship, hit the rocks of Catterage. Henry's heart was broken: he left his Kingdom to his daughter, Mathilda. The seeds of Civil War were sown and the reaping would be bitter. Walter Tirel stayed in France and never returned. He swore on his deathbed, on his own immortal soul, that he had not even seen the Red King that fateful Lammas morrow so many years ago. In the end, God's truth will be known. I leave it now. I turn and look out the window at the herbarium and the bench where I and my master sat so many years ago. What fear do I have of death? – I want to walk with him in God's own light. Heaven is friendship ...

VII & VIII

Vespers and Compline
Historical Notes

Walter Tirel never returned to England. He must have been a very frightened man. Abbot Suger of St Denis in his *Life of Louis VI* maintains that "he had often heard Tirel, at a time when he had nothing to hope or fear, affirm on the solemnest oath that on the fateful day he neither went into that part of the wood where the King was nor even caught sight of him in the wood", (Abbot Suger, *Vie de Louis VI le Gros*, edited and translated by H. Waquet, [Paris 1929, 1964], p.12.) John Salisbury, who rewrote Eadmer's *Life of Anselm*, maintains that Tirel, on his deathbed invoking God's judgement on his eternal soul, proclaimed his total innocence and "that the King himself" had loosed the fatal arrow, (John of Salisbury, *Vita Sancti Anselm*, Patrologia Latina, CXXIX 1031). Tirel was a friend of Anselm's: Rigg, in his biography of the saint, describes how Tirel once hosted a banquet for Anselm but there was a shortage of fish. Anselm assured his host that more fish was on its way to Walter's Castle. A short while later two men appeared carrying a lovely, freshly caught sturgeon, (J.M. Rigg, *Anselm* [Methuen, 1896], p.41).

Accordingly, we have two eminent primary sources, Suger and John Salisbury who very distinctly declare that Tirel, even on his deathbed, maintained his total innocence in any involvement in the Red King's death. In the 12th century, such solemn oaths, particularly at death's door, must be regarded as crucial evidence. Tirel's words must be taken at face value. He wasn't in the same part of the wood as the King – indeed he never saw him. These two sources are strengthened by a third, Eadmer himself. Tirel was known both to him and Anselm. Eadmer, who had no love for the Red King, could have depicted Tirel as God's agent in this matter, yet he never does. Eadmer never mentions Tirel and it is no coincidence that John of Salisbury, when rewriting Eadmer's *Life of Anselm*, categorically repeats Tirel's clear statement on the killing of 2nd August, 1100. Indeed Tirel's remark on how the King himself loosed the fatal arrow, does not make sense unless he is referring not to Rufus, but Henry I. The actual phrase is "Qui ipsium regem jaculum quo interemptus est misisse". The naming of Ralph (Radulphus de Aquis) (or Aix) occurs in the *Liber de Principis Instructione* – A Book concerning the Instruction of a Prince – written by Giraldus Cambriensis – Gerald of Wales, edited by G.F. Warner in his *Giraldi Cambriensis Opera* (Rolls Series) Volume VIII, (1891), pp.324-25. Gerald gives two versions of Rufus' death: the first is that Rufus was killed by a chance 'bolt' by one of his own men. In the second version Gerald of Wales describes how the Prior of Dunstable had a vision that the Red King was bound for God's judgement. The Prior, as in other stories, sees a beautiful virgin pleading with the Lord Jesus, when suddenly the Prior also sees a man "Niger et Hispidus" (black and rough) approach the Red King and offer some arrows: the Lord Jesus declares that one of the these arrows will be his vengeance on Rufus. The Prior hurries to the Red King in the New Forest to warn him when he glimpses the very man he saw in his vision present the King with those arrows to whom Rufus returns some of them. They both go off hunting and this man, Ralph de Aquis, looses one of the arrows which kills Rufus. Now Gerald's story is similar to the visions of other monks and Abbot Serlo's warnings, whilst Dunstable Abbey was not founded till the reign of Henry I. However, Gerald was a royal clerk and courtier during the reign of Henry II. He never mentions Tirel but this Ralph de Aquis, (which, according to all the topographical surveys, must be Bath – again another place in the south-west of England where so much agitation regarding Rufus' death originated). Gerald had nothing to lose by naming Tirel, but again he is a contemporary of Abbot Suger and John of Salisbury. The reign of Henry I is over and, perhaps, the truth about Tirel's involvement in Rufus' death is beginning to emerge. What is also interesting is that Gerald does focus on the story by Oderic Vitalis regarding the presentation of arrows to Rufus, an act of deep significance for the events of 2nd August, 1100.

I have searched high and low for Ralph de Aquis but the only reference I have found is to a royal huntsman/archer Ralph named by Barlow, *William Rufus* (Methuen, 1983), pp.126 and 128.

In conclusion, I find it very difficult to accept the conclusion of Barlow and others that the Red King's death was an accident. They cite an article by the historian Warren C. Hollister and maintain Professor Hollister totally disproved the conspiracy theory (C.W. Hollister, 'The Strange Death of William Rufus', *Speculum*, XlVIII, [1973]). This is not true. Hollister merely criticises one conspiracy theory, and a very weak one, advanced by Grinnell Milne, *The Killing of William Rufus*, that Tirel was acting for his kinsmen, the de Clares. Hollister dismisses this, and I agree with him, but that does not mean there was not a conspiracy. Historians emphasise the importance of Robert Curthose's imminent return but they underestimate the power of the Papacy, Anselm's stance and how Robert's return would activate this. Anselm had been Pope Urban II's special guest at the Easter Synod of 1099 which gathered around the tomb of St Peter in Rome. At that meeting Anselm was supported by Renier, Bishop of Lucca: Eadmer, *Historia Novorum in Anglia*, pp.116-18, whilst Urban's successor, Paschal II, was obdurate in defending

Anselm's claims. Schmitt, *Sancti Anselm Opera Omnia*, letters 222, 223. Papal envoys did arrive in England in 1100 but quickly withdrew: Eadmer, *Historia Novorum in Anglia*, p.126.

The other historical details mentioned here can be found in Barlow, Vaughan and Strickland. On the Ansfrida story: *Chronicon Monasterii de Abingdon*, ed. J. Stevenson, (Rolls Series, 1858), pp.36-9. On Meulan's daughter, Isabel being Henry's mistress: Freeman, *The Reign of William Rufus*, (1882), II, p.380. I have placed Eadmer's death as late as some authorities allow, c.1140. The fate of all the main protagonists are as he describes. Eadmer himself continued to serve at Canterbury. He was, at one time, nominated as a possible Archbishop in Scotland but this was never confirmed due to the age-old problem regarding the power of the Archbishop of Canterbury to consecrate all bishops in these islands.

Finally I would like to refer to Emma Mason's excellent book which was published whilst I was finishing mine. *William II, Rufus, the Red King* is an excellent scholarly study. However, I must disagree with Miss Mason's theory behind the Red King's death (although it was refreshing to see another historian reject the accident theory).

© Paul C Doherty
February, 2006

www.paulcdoherty.com

GREENWICH EXCHANGE BOOKS

The previous book in this series by Paul Doherty
The Secret Life of Elizabeth I
was published by Greenwich Exchange ealier in this year.
It was the subject of a major television programme.

LITERATURE & BIOGRAPHY

Matthew Arnold and 'Thyrsis' *by Patrick Carill Connolly*
Matthew Arnold (1822-1888) was a leading poet, intellect and aesthete of the Victorian epoch. He is now best known for his strictures as a literary and cultural critic, and educationist. After a long period of neglect, his views have come in for a re-evaluation. Arnold's poetry remains less well known, yet his poems and his understanding of poetry, which defied the conventions of his time, were central to his achievement.
The author traces Arnold's intellectual and poetic development, showing how his poetry gathers its meanings from a lifetime's study of European literature and philosophy. Connolly's unique exegesis of 'Thyrsis' draws upon a wide-ranging analysis of the pastoral and its associated myths in both classical and native cultures. This study shows lucidly and in detail how Arnold encouraged the intense reflection of the mind on the subject placed before it, believing in " … the all importance of the choice of the subject, the necessity of accurate observation; and subordinate character of expression."
Patrick Carill Connolly gained his English degree at Reading University and taught English literature abroad for a number of years before returning to Britain. He is now a civil servant living in London.
2004 • 180 pages • ISBN 1-871551-61-7

The Author, the Book and the Reader *by Robert Giddings*
This collection of essays analyses the effects of changing technology and the attendant commercial pressures on literary styles and subject matter. Authors covered include Charles Dickens, Tobias Smollett, Mark Twain, Dr Johnson and John le Carré.
1991 • 220 pages • illustrated • ISBN 1-871551-01-3

Body of Truth
D.H. Lawrence: The Nomadic Years, 1919-1930 *by Philip Callow*
This book provides a fresh insight into Lawrence's art as well as his life. Candid about the relationship between Lawrence and his wife, it shows nevertheless the strength of the bond between them. If no other book persuaded the reader of Lawrence's greatness, this does.
Philip Callow – biographer, novelist, and poet – has also written lives of Chekhov, Cézanne, Robert Louis Stevenson, Walt Whitman and Van Gogh all publishedto critical acclaim. His biography of D.H. Lawrence's early years, *Son and Lover*, was widely praised.
2006 • 286 pages • ISBN 1-871551-82-X

Aleister Crowley and the Cult of Pan *by Paul Newman*
Few more nightmarish figures stalk English literature than Aleister Crowley (1875-1947), poet, magician, mountaineer and agent provocateur. In this groundbreaking study, Paul Newman dives into the occult mire of Crowley's works and fishes out gems and grotesqueries that are by turns ethereal, sublime, pornographic and horrifying. Like Oscar Wilde before him, Crowley stood in "symbolic relationship to his age" and to contemporaries like Rupert Brooke, G.K. Chesterton and the Portuguese modernist, Fernando Pessoa. An influential exponent of the cult of the Great God Pan, his essentially 'pagan' outlook was shared by major European writers as well as English novelists like E.M. Forster, D.H. Lawrence and Arthur Machen.
Paul Newman lives in Cornwall. Editor of the literary magazine *Abraxas*, he has written over ten books.
2004 • 222 pages • ISBN 1-871551-66-8

John Dryden *by Anthony Fowles*
Of all the poets of the Augustan age, John Dryden was the most worldly. Anthony Fowles traces Dryden's evolution from 'wordsmith' to major poet. This critical study shows a poet of vigour and technical panache whose art was forged in the heat and battle of a turbulent polemical and pamphleteering age. Although Dryden's status as a literary critic has long been established, Fowles draws attention to his neglected achievements as a translator of poetry. He deals also with the less well-known aspects of Dryden's work – his plays and occasional pieces.
Born in London and educated at the Universities of Oxford and Southern California, Anthony Fowles began his career in film-making before becoming an author of film and television scripts and more than twenty books. Readers will welcome the many contemporary references to novels and film with which Fowles illuminates the life and work of this decisively influential English poetic voice.
2003 • 292 pages • ISBN 1-871551-58-7

The Good That We Do *by John Lucas*
John Lucas' book blends fiction, biography and social history in order to tell the story of his grandfather, Horace Kelly. Headteacher of a succession of elementary schools in impoverished areas of London, 'Hod' Kelly was also a keen cricketer, a devotee of the music hall, and included among his friends the great trade union leader Ernest Bevin. In telling the story of his life, Lucas has provided a fascinating range of insights into the lives of ordinary Londoners from the First World War until the outbreak of the Second World War. Threaded throughout is an account of such people's hunger for education, and of the different ways government, church and educational officialdom ministered to that hunger. *The Good That We Do* is both a study of one man and of a period when England changed, drastically and forever.
John Lucas is Professor Emeritus of the Universities of Loughborough and Nottingham Trent. He is the author of numerous works of a critical and scholarly nature and has published seven collections of poetry.
2001 • 214 pages • ISBN 1-871551-54-4

In Pursuit of Lewis Carroll *by Raphael Shaberman*
Sherlock Holmes and the author uncover new evidence in their investigations into the mysterious life and writing of Lewis Carroll. They examine published works by Carroll that have been overlooked by previous commentators. A newly-discovered poem, almost certainly by Carroll, is published here.
Amongst many aspects of Carroll's highly complex personality, this book explores his relationship with his parents, numerous child friends, and the formidable Mrs Liddell, mother of the immortal Alice. Raphael Shaberman was a founder member of the Lewis Carroll Society and a teacher of autistic children.
1994 • 118 pages • illustrated • ISBN 1-871551-13-7

Liar! Liar!: Jack Kerouac – Novelist *by R.J. Ellis*
The fullest study of Jack Kerouac's fiction to date. It is the first book to devote an individual chapter to every one of his novels. *On the Road*, *Visions of Cody* and *The Subterraneans* are reread in-depth, in a new and exciting way. *Visions of Gerard* and *Doctor Sax* are also strikingly reinterpreted, as are other daringly innovative writings, like 'The Railroad Earth' and his "try at a spontaneous *Finnegans Wake*" – *Old Angel Midnight*. Neglected writings, such as *Tristessa* and *Big Sur*, are also analysed, alongside better-known novels such as *Dharma Bums* and *Desolation Angels*.
R.J. Ellis is Senior Lecturer in English at Nottingham Trent University.
1999 • 294 pages • ISBN 1-871551-53-6

Musical Offering *by Yolanthe Leigh*
In a series of vivid sketches, anecdotes and reflections, Yolanthe Leigh tells the story of her growing up in the Poland of the 1930s and the Second World War. These are poignant episodes of a child's first encounters with both the enchantments and the cruelties of the world; and from a later time, stark memories of the brutality of the Nazi invasion, and the hardships of student life in Warsaw under the Occupation. But most of all this is a record of inward development; passages of remarkable intensity and simplicity describe the girl's response to religion, to music, and to her discovery of philosophy.
Yolanthe Leigh was formerly a Lecturer in Philosophy at Reading University.
2000 • 56 pages • ISBN: 1-871551-46-3

Norman Cameron *by Warren Hope*
Norman Cameron's poetry was admired by W.H. Auden, celebrated by Dylan Thomas and valued by Robert Graves. He was described by Martin Seymour-Smith as, "one of … the most rewarding and pure poets of his generation …" and is at last given a full-length biography. This eminently sociable man, who had periods of darkness and despair, wrote little poetry by comparison with others of his time, but it is always of a consistently high quality – imaginative and profound.
2000 • 220 pages • illustrated • ISBN 1-871551-05-6

POETRY

Adam's Thoughts in Winter *by Warren Hope*
Warren Hope's poems have appeared from time to time in a number of literary periodicals, pamphlets and anthologies on both sides of the Atlantic. They appeal to lovers of poetry everywhere. His poems are brief, clear, frequently lyrical, characterised by wit, but often distinguished by tenderness. The poems gathered in this first book-length collection counter the brutalising ethos of contemporary life, speaking of, and for, the virtues of modesty, honesty and gentleness in an individual, memorable way.
2000 • 46 pages • ISBN 1-871551-40-4

Baudelaire: Les Fleurs du Mal *Translated by F.W. Leakey*
Selected poems from *Les Fleurs du Mal* are translated with parallel French texts and are designed to be read with pleasure by readers who have no French as well as those who are practised in the French language.
F.W. Leakey was Professor of French in the University of London. As a scholar, critic and teacher he specialised in the work of Baudelaire for 50 years and published a number of books on the poet.
2001 • 152 pages • ISBN 1-871551-10-2

'The Last Blackbird' and other poems by Ralph Hodgson *edited and introduced by John Harding*
Ralph Hodgson (1871-1962) was a poet and illustrator whose most influential and enduring work appeared to great acclaim just prior to, and during, the First World War. His work is imbued with a spiritual passion for the beauty of creation and the mystery of existence. This new selection brings together, for the first time in 40 years, some of the most beautiful and powerful 'hymns to life' in the English language.
John Harding lives in London. He is a freelance writer and teacher and is Ralph Hodgson's biographer.
2004 • 70 pages • ISBN 1-871551-81-1

Lines from the Stone Age *by Sean Haldane*
Reviewing Sean Haldane's 1992 volume *Desire in Belfast*, Robert Nye wrote in *The Times* that "Haldane can be sure of his place among the English poets." This place is not yet a conspicuous one, mainly because his early volumes appeared in Canada, and because he has earned his living by other means than literature. Despite this, his poems have always had their circle of readers. The 60 previously unpublished poems of *Lines from the Stone Age* – "lines of longing, terror, pride, lust and pain" – may widen this circle.
2000 • 52 pages • ISBN 1-871551-39-0

Martin Seymour-Smith – Collected Poems *edited by Peter Davies* (180pp)
To the general public Martin Seymour-Smith (1928-1998) is known as a distinguished literary biographer, notably of Robert Graves, Rudyard Kipling and Thomas Hardy. To such figures as John Dover Wilson, William Empson, Stephen Spender and Anthony Burgess, he was regarded as one of the most independently-minded scholars of his generation, through his pioneering critical edition of Shakespeare's *Sonnets*, and his magisterial *Guide to Modern World Literature*.
To his fellow poets, Graves, James Reeves, C.H. Sisson and Robert Nye – he was first and foremost a poet. As this collection demonstrates, at the centre of the poems is a passionate engagement with Man, his sexuality and his personal relationships.
2006 • 182 pages • ISBN 1-871551-47-1

The Rain and the Glass *by Robert Nye*
When Robert Nye's first poems were published, G.S. Fraser declared in the *Times Literary Supplement*: "Here is a proper poet, though it is hard to see how the larger literary public (greedy for flattery of their own concerns) could be brought to recognize that. But other proper poets – how many of them are left? – will recognize one of themselves."

Since then Nye has become known to a large public for his novels, especially *Falstaff* (1976), winner of the Hawthornden Prize and The Guardian Fiction Prize, and *The Late Mr Shakespeare* (1998). But his true vocation has always been poetry, and it is as a poet that he is best known to his fellow poets. "Nye is the inheritor of a poetic tradition that runs from Donne and Ralegh to Edward Thomas and Robert Graves," wrote James Aitchison in 1990, while the critic Gabriel Josipovici has described him as "one of the most interesting poets writing today, with a voice unlike that of any of his contemporaries".

This book contains all the poems Nye has written since his *Collected Poems* of 1995, together with his own selection from that volume. An introduction, telling the story of his poetic beginnings, affirms Nye's unfashionable belief in inspiration, as well as defining that quality of unforced truth which distinguishes the best of his work: "I have spent my life trying to write poems, but the poems gathered here came mostly when I was not."
2005 • 132 pages • ISBN 1-871551-41-2

Wilderness by *Martin Seymour-Smith*
This is Martin Seymour-Smith's first publication of his poetry for more than twenty years. This collection of 36 poems is a fearless account of an inner life of love, frustration, guilt, laughter and the celebration of others. He is best known to the general public as the author of the controversial and bestselling *Hardy* (1994).
1994 • 52 pages • ISBN 1-871551-08-0

STUDENT GUIDE LITERARY SERIES

The Greenwich Exchange Student Guide Literary Series is a collection of critical essays of major or contemporary serious writers in English and selected European languages. The series is for the student, the teacher and 'common readers' and is an ideal resource for libraries. The *Times Educational Supplement* praised these books, saying, "The style of [this series] has a pressure of meaning behind it. Readers should learn from that ... If art is about selection, perception and taste, then this is it."

(ISBN prefix 1-871551- applies)
All books are paperbacks unless otherwise stated

The series includes:
W.H. Auden by Stephen Wade (36-6)
Honoré de Balzac by Wendy Mercer (48-X)
William Blake by Peter Davies (27-7)

The Brontës by Peter Davies (24-2)
Robert Browning by John Lucas (59-5)
Lord Byron by Andrew Keanie (83-9)
Samuel Taylor Coleridge by Andrew Keanie (64-1)
Joseph Conrad by Martin Seymour-Smith (18-8)
William Cowper by Michael Thorn (25-0)
Charles Dickens by Robert Giddings (26-9)
Emily Dickinson by Marnie Pomeroy (68-4)
John Donne by Sean Haldane (23-4)
Ford Madox Ford by Anthony Fowles (63-3)
The Stagecraft of Brian Friel by David Grant (74-9)
Robert Frost by Warren Hope (70-6)
Thomas Hardy by Sean Haldane (33-1)
Seamus Heaney by Warren Hope (37-4)
Joseph Heller by Anthony Fowles (84-6)
Gerard Manley Hopkins by Sean Sheehan (77-3)
James Joyce by Michael Murphy (73-0)
Laughter in the Dark – The Plays of Joe Orton by Arthur Burke (56-0)
Philip Larkin by Warren Hope (35-8)
Sylvia Plath by Marnie Pomeroy (88-9)
Poets of the First World War by John Greening (79-X)
Philip Roth by Paul McDonald (72-2)
Shakespeare's *A Midsummer Night's Dream* by Matt Simpson (90-0)
Shakespeare's *King Lear* by Peter Davies (95-1)
Shakespeare's *Macbeth* by Matt Simpson (69-2)
Shakespeare's *Othello* by Matt Simpson (71-4)
Shakespeare's *The Tempest* by Matt Simpson (75-7)
Shakespeare's *Twelfth Night* by Matt Simpson (86-2)
Shakespeare's Non-Dramatic Poetry by Martin Seymour-Smith (22-6)
Shakespeare's Sonnets by Martin Seymour-Smith (38-2)
Shakespeare's *The Winter's Tale* by John Lucas (80-3)
Tobias Smollett by Robert Giddings (21-8)
Dylan Thomas by Peter Davies (78-1)
Alfred, Lord Tennyson by Michael Thorn (20-X)
William Wordsworth by Andrew Keanie (57-9)
W.B. Yeats by John Greening (34-X)